Praise for

Highgate Shifters

I liked this book. The writing was well done and fast paced. I enjoyed how the book was more emotionally driven than just about the sex... An enjoyable read and I look forward to reading more in this series.
~ *MM Good Book Reviews*

This is a very good read! I never once got lost, but there are loose ends that can only be resolved by the next installment. The ending made my heart break but it also made me just want more and more out of this. Me. Likey! ~ *Multitasking Mommas*

I0542057

Totally Bound Publishing books by Sydney Presley:

Highgate Shifters
Jace's Justice
Vann's Victory

HIGHGATE SHIFTERS
Volume One

Jace's Justice

Vann's Victory

SYDNEY PRESLEY

Highgate Shifters Volume One
ISBN # 978-1-78430-402-7
©Copyright Sydney Presley 2015
Cover Art by Posh Gosh ©Copyright 2015
Interior text design by Claire Siemaszkiewicz
Totally Bound Publishing

Published in 2015 by Totally Bound Publishing, Newland House, The Point, Weaver Road, Lincoln, LN6 3QN, United Kingdom.

Totally Bound Publishing is a subsidiary of Totally Entwined Group Limited.

JACE'S JUSTICE

Chapter One

The sound of the whip-poor-will gave Jace the willies. He could only hope that sometime in the future Louie would give him the willies too, but he didn't think that was about to happen any time soon. To have Louie's cock inside him—God, that was a dream. Louie hadn't given him any indication he fancied him in *that* way, more was the pity.

Yeah, a massive pity. No use even thinking about it. Can't change it. Well, I could, but if I tell Louie how I feel I'll end up embarrassed when Louie tells me to fuck off. Because he will *tell me to fuck off.*

He shrugged off the thoughts, telling himself to buck the hell up. Pining wasn't really Jace's thing, but he was close to pining now. He usually dealt with issues internally, making out that nothing bothered him, although it did. His scowls and short answers let the rest of the pack know he wasn't to be approached unless they wanted their heads bitten off.

He laughed, imagining biting their heads off literally. Sergeant, the alpha, would have something to say about that. And upsetting Sergeant wasn't something Jace wanted to do. The man had been good to him — to everyone.

Jace sighed. The ache in his torso was almost too much to bear. It reminded him of Louie again, not that the man was ever far from his thoughts. Being near Louie so often on a daily basis, even though they didn't talk much beyond hello or a casual sentence or two… Well, that was killing him.

Could a wolf shifter die from never uniting with his mate?

And Louie *was* Jace's mate, no doubt about that. Jace felt it in his goddamn bones. It was just a shame Louie didn't feel it too. Or if he did, he hadn't shown it. Louie acted like any other pack member, nothing more. No 'accidental' touches, no secret looks across the room.

"Shit."

Jace stood on the rear porch of the main pack house and stared out at the compound. He ought to go for a run, really. Shift and streak around until he was out of breath. He had to do something to get this feeling of restlessness out of him. This feeling of loving someone who didn't return the emotions. How long should he wait? That was the question — the very big question that loomed over him each and every day. How long would it be before Louie got that smack of emotion in his chest where he realized they were meant to be together? That they were mates? Intended for one another since birth?

"How fucking long?"

I'll wait forever if I have to. I can't imagine being with anyone else. Can't be with anyone else.

It seemed Jace *had* been waiting forever, that he'd loved Louie forever — and he had. The longing inside him had grown to massive proportions, threatening to swallow him whole.

He wished Louie would swallow him whole.

"Enough with that crap," he muttered.

To stop himself thinking of innuendoes, Jace stripped out of his clothes then put them in one of the clothes bins on the porch. He stood with no care that someone might see him naked. It was commonplace on pack lands for men and women to stroll nude before or after a shift, completely at ease with their bodies and who they were—*what* they were. What Jace had to be mindful of was getting a hard-on when Louie stripped in front of him. And *Louie* not getting hard was surely an indication he didn't fancy Jace. Jace had never seen Louie's cock as anything but flaccid, so if Louie had feelings for Jace, he was damn good at controlling his emotions. Then again, Louie always got dressed quickly, with his back turned to anyone who was there. A few times Jace had hoped that was because Louie was hiding one hell of a hard-on, but there never was a bulge in his jeans when he turned round fully clothed.

If Jace and Louie were meant to be together, why hadn't it happened yet? They were well into adulthood. Most wolves, as far as he'd seen growing up, had got together during puberty. Then again, there were a few who had mated later in life.

So there's hope yet.

But what if fate had got it all wrong? What if a humungous mistake had been made and Jace was destined to spend the rest of his life without ever bonding with Louie?

I can't do it. I'll have to go to another compound or one of the institutes. No way can I live here and watch Louie with someone else.

Then again, there couldn't *be* anyone else for Louie. Could there? Jace might have read his feelings wrong. He could have just assumed that the love he felt for Louie *was* love, when really it was only his longings. And that might well be it. Jace had never loved anyone else so had nothing to compare it to. He had no blood parents that he knew of, having been taken in as an abandoned cub at a day old, or so Sergeant had said. Jace supposed he should love Sergeant, but he didn't think he did. He was grateful for being brought up on these beautiful lands by him, grateful for being fed and clothed, but the kind of abiding love a kid should feel for a parent wasn't there.

In short, Jace had never really belonged.

Before he gave in to more maudlin thoughts, he stepped off the porch and onto the grass. It prickled the soles of his feet, and the familiar brush of it brought with it a stronger desire to shift. It had always been that way, with the touch of grass, and he couldn't fight it any longer. He relaxed his muscles, held his arms out, tilted his face to the night sky and waited for the transformation to take place.

In his wolf skin, he always felt so different— liberated, somewhat excited, exhilaration streaming through him that he was at one with his inner self. He embraced that now, shucking his fur-covered skin so it rippled down his new form then finally settled into place. He scented the air, digging his claws into the ground. The dampness of it seeped into his pads, infusing him with the need to bolt, to run so fast he lost the ability to breathe.

So he ran, shooting across the vast lawn toward the row of oaks that stood soldier-like, guarding the entrance to the woods beyond. Once at the oaks, he slowed a little, senses on high alert for interlopers—

wolf or human. Other animals, well, they were welcome.

The oaks gave way to pines and birches, white ash and shadbush, the foliage spouting thickly from arthritic branches. Those branches didn't start until quite a way up the trunks, higher than a six-foot man. What faced Jace were row upon row of trunks, something he had long known how to navigate, the paths created between them made from years of shifters padding through the woods. He ran on, dodging, weaving—he could do that with his eyes closed. His lungs burned, his ribcage fit to burst, yet still he plowed on.

He wouldn't stop until the ache in his chest had eased.

Will it ever ease, though?

That was another insistent question he asked himself regularly. He shook it off, planning to concentrate on the run, the thrill of it and nothing else. He huffed out a breath that was accompanied by a rough growl. In human form it would have been a laugh of derision.

Concentrate on nothing else? Chance would be a fine thing. Since when have I ever been able to get Louie out of my mind? He's always there. The sight of him. His voice…

If he could have shouted 'fuck my life' he would have. Instead, he howled, long and high-pitched, a distress call if ever there was one. If another shifter came running to see what the matter was, they'd wonder why he'd called out, seeing as he was still running and probably looked like he was fine. He'd have to lie, tell them he'd stood on a thorn. The truth wasn't anything he could admit to—unless it was to Louie, but that was debatable if he'd ever even do that. To save anyone coming to his aid, he howled again, a low, steady sound that said he was okay.

But he wasn't okay and never would be until—

Until? Admit it. Until Louie wakes the fuck up. If he ever does.

But he had to, otherwise Jace would find himself either eaten up with his inability to express his feelings or living on another compound. And who was to say he'd be welcomed elsewhere? Yeah, relations between compounds were relatively good, but shifters moving from one to the other wasn't encouraged. The institutes were a different matter. Halfway houses, that's what they were. Places for shifters who didn't belong to any packs. Some were also used to incarcerate shifter felons.

'You belong where you're brought up,' Sergeant was fond of saying.

Well, fuck you, Sergeant. I wasn't meant to be here. I didn't ask to be here.

He chastised himself for being a selfish prick. Sergeant hadn't been obliged to take Jace in—he'd done so out of the goodness of his heart. Jace could have been left to starve on the side of the country road that led to the compound. Sergeant could have decided to take a different path for his run that night, bypassing Jace and never knowing that the cub had existed.

But he didn't, and now I'm here, always feeling out of place, an extra.

Jace ran on, the thud of his paws reverberating through his body every time he smacked them onto the ground. Those thuds went some way to calming him, and he admitted he was a selfish bastard at times for thinking the way he did. But with no one to really express himself to, what else could he do? If he didn't sort through the muddle of thoughts in his head he'd go mad.

Tell Louie how I feel?

Jace shuddered and thrust that thought out of his head. He didn't fancy opening up, not when Louie might rebuff him. He couldn't risk the world of hurt he'd find himself in if he were rejected. That would sting like a son of a bitch.

The scent of another wolf drifted over him, and Jace immediately slowed to a stop. His heart rate sped up, the pulse of it thundering in his ears. He panted, the rattle of his breaths drowning out every other forest sound for a long moment. He wedged himself between two tree trunks then sat so it would appear he was part of the scenery. The aroma was coming from ahead, so he narrowed his eyes, seeking out movement in the darkness. The moon was shrouded in cloud coverage tonight, so his vision was limited despite it being sharper when he was in wolf form.

Nothing moved.

He cocked his head, straining to hear better now that his breathing had almost returned to normal.

He heard nothing unusual.

Deciding to leave his hiding place, he padded forward, spotting the clearing up ahead that gave him a chance to rest, where he usually sprawled out on the grass. There was a pool there, and most nights he shifted back to human form so he could bathe in the cool water. Then he'd spend time on his back, staring at the stars and wishing Louie was there with him.

At the edge of the clearing, low growling caught his attention. His hackles rose, and he resisted the urge to sneeze — the foreign scent was so strong, invading him with its tang. Yet it was a tang similar to his own — one that didn't belong here, just like him. Another scent arrived, so familiar that it almost erased Jace's concentration.

Louie.

Another growl, one he'd heard a million times, a warning for the stranger shifter not to come closer. But where were they? Jace scanned the trees bordering the clearing, seeing nothing but goddamn trunks, leaves and murky shadows.

Show yourself, stranger. Come on, step out.

Jace felt altogether braver now he knew Louie was there somewhere—bolder, more able to handle the running off of an unwelcome wolf on the property. Together they could handle whoever it was should 'whoever' turn nasty.

Louie appeared first, coming out of the woods on the opposite side of the pool. He raised his head—*so damn regal*—and sniffed. His fur would have glittered had the moon been allowed to shine. Louie's pelt always looked like the dark strands were made of fiber optics, silver-tipped at the ends. When he shrugged into his wolf skin after a shift, it sparkled much like the stars Jace loved to stare at.

Maybe that was why he liked staring at them.

Now wasn't the time to entertain such things, though. There was a possible fight on the horizon, and Jace needed to keep his wits about him, be there for Louie if all hell broke loose.

The stranger emerged from the trees opposite Louie and to Jace's right. If all their positions were joined by lines they'd form a triangle, the still waters of the pool at the center. The new wolf didn't have glittery fur. It was dull with sweat and maybe even dirt, as though the animal had been traveling for a long time. Weariness, that was what emanated from the beast— and a beast it was. Large, standing almost half a foot higher than either Jace or Louie. Although the animal was a little on the skinny side, Jace knew it had once been wide and well fed.

How do I know that?

Jace sniffed, taking in a long pull of air, drawing that alien yet familiar scent into him. It smelled like home. Yeah, if he knew what home smelled like, that would be it. Confused and unsure what to do, Jace waited for Louie to make the first move. Louie would have scented Jace, would know he didn't have to fight alone if that's what this confrontation came to.

The foreigner suddenly shifted, changing into a man so tall Jace estimated him to be more than a few inches higher than himself. Jace stared, blinking at the sight.

The man looked just like Jace. His hair was longer, wavier, the tips brushing his shoulders, but it held the same dark brown shade. The body...well, it was broader, more sinewy, the belly dipping inwards a bit where he possibly hadn't taken much food onboard.

A mark on the man's chest brought Jace up short.

What the fuck?

Jace forced himself to see more clearly.

The mark was the same as his own, a crude cross like a kiss at the end of a love letter. Jace had always thought his had been made by branches gouging into his skin when he'd been dumped on the roadside. It wasn't likely that two cubs had been marked the exact same way.

Not unless someone deliberately cut us... No, that's just stupid. It's a coincidence, that's all.

"Listen," the man said. "I mean you no harm. I'm just here—" He paused to take in a breath. "Just here to find someone. My name's Vann. If you could answer a question for me before I go on my way?"

Louie shifted then stood there, the sight of him sending Jace weak at the knees.

Not now, damn it. Don't let him affect you this way now.

"What do you want to know?" Louie asked, his chest, leg and pubic hair similar to his wolf fur. He flicked his head to move a strand that hovered over his eye—no white tips on his head, just pure black goodness.

"You might not know the answer, but I have nothing to lose," Vann said. He shrugged, gave a smile that showed his fatigue. "I'm here to find my brother. Dropped on the roadside twenty-five years ago as a cub. I have to speak to him. I can't rest until I've found him."

Jace's vision misted. A ball of emotion mixed with panic lodged in his throat. It couldn't be him Vann was looking for. There must have been a mistake. The shift took over Jace without warning then he stood there on shaking human legs before stumbling from the trees and into the clearing. He felt sick and battled against vomiting.

This isn't happening.

He registered Louie glancing his way, took in the fact that Vann was staring at him, the look on his face probably the same as the one on Jace's. One of shock. He had pale skin and his mouth was slightly open. Jace was highly aware that this Vann had so much to say but that nothing was coming out, much like Jace himself.

And he also acknowledged the ground coming up to greet his face—and there was no energy in him to stop it.

Chapter Two

"Stay the hell away from him," Louie yelled as he skirted the pool, heading toward Jace.

This Vann had no business being near Jace, and Louie was fucked if he'd let him get within an inch of him. Strangers at Highgate compound weren't the norm, and as for a wolf being here—well, that spoke of trouble. And as for Jace fainting...

What the fuck was all that about?

Jace had always appeared so strong, like nothing fazed him.

Fear wended through Louie at the thought that the day he'd always dreaded had finally come. Someone had arrived to claim Jace as one of their pack. Images of Jace being spirited away jostled in Louie's mind, and it was all he could do to stop himself from shouting out his anger and pain. And shit, he *was* in pain. It nipped at his nerves, flooding his system until he thought his body would splinter from it.

I should be used to that by now. I feel this way at least once every day when it comes to Jace.

He ran the short distance to Jace then flung himself down on his knees beside him. A quick check proved Jace was alive, but whether he was well or not remained to be seen. Jace was out cold, sweat beading his forehead and temples, soaking the roots of his hair. He shivered too.

"He's in fucking shock," Louie muttered, taking hold of Jace beneath his armpits so he could drag him to the pool.

He sensed the stranger approaching, and if he'd been in wolf form, Louie's hackles would have been well and truly up.

"I said stay the hell away," Louie ground out, glancing over his shoulder to see where the man was.

Vann stood a few meters away at the pool edge, his face so much like Jace's it freaked Louie out. Okay, there were subtle differences, but if it wasn't for Vann's height, anyone could mistake him for Jace in the darkness. He even smelled similar, for fuck's sake. There was no denying it. Unless Vann's features were a massive fluke, this man was related to Jace.

Shit. I should have let Jace know how I feel. Should have told him before…

It was probably too late now. Once Jace woke and recovered from the shock, he'd be excited to know he had family. He'd go with this intruder, back to wherever the hell Vann had come from, and meet other people.

Other possible mates.

Louie held back a groan of agony, reminding himself that there couldn't *be* any other mates. Not true ones who were destined to be together like he and Jace were. Some shifters joined up with others when they weren't true, but they had to be unhappy deep down, didn't they?

He couldn't force Jace to like him—to love him—although he'd seen the way Jace had looked at him sometimes when he'd thought Louie wasn't watching. Yeah, Jace was attracted to him, that much was certain—it was obvious from the way he watched Louie—but as for love? No.

Concentrate on what's going on here. Don't let your thoughts wander when there's a stranger on the compound.

Once at the pool edge, Louie made sure Vann was in front of him as he positioned Jace on his side, facing Louie. All the man would see of Jace's privates was his bare ass. The rest, the parts Louie wished he'd been intimate with, were safety hidden from Vann's view.

"Keep away," Louie said, leaning across to scoop some water into his hands. It was cold, and an involuntary shiver shuddered through his body.

"Don't worry, I will," Vann said.

Louie had expected a tinge of sarcasm, maybe irritation, but all he'd heard was a quivering statement that rang of Vann being somewhat afraid. Louie didn't for one second think his countenance had anything to do with that. No, Vann would be afraid that he'd been the cause of Jace collapsing. And he fucking was.

Bastard. Why did you have to come here?

Louie knew the answer. Pretending he didn't was stupid. If he'd been Vann, he'd have done the same thing. Making sure your family were safe and cared for was a must. Sergeant had drilled it into everyone that you looked after your own. Although Louie had never been to another compound, he was sure they all worked the same way. Wherever Vann was from, whoever the alpha was there, he had probably brought them all up telling them the same stuff Sergeant told the Highgate pack.

Louie dribbled water over Jace's cheeks, hoping the sudden cold would startle him awake. After the first scoopful of water had no positive result, he collected more, going for the abrupt splash instead. Jace spluttered, snapping his eyes open and looking directly up at Louie. Jace smiled, as if he'd forgotten why he was on the ground, and it was a perfect moment where time was suspended and nothing else mattered. Then Jace's memory must have kicked in. His face changed from a serene expression to one of panicked horror, then changed again to something akin to hope.

Shit. He'll be wanting to leave me, then. To go with Vann and start a new life.

Louie swallowed down the hurt. "You all right?"

"That guy…?" Jace struggled to sit up.

Louie gave him a hand. "He's over there," he whispered. "He looks like you, man. Do you think…?"

"I don't know what to think." Jace moved so he faced Vann but sat beside Louie. He went on. "It's no secret we have an orphan in our pack," he said to Vann. "Why should we believe you? You could be anyone." He stared at him, clearly taking in that scar on the guy's chest.

"Not with this, I'm not." Vann pressed a finger to his cross, taking a step closer.

"Back the fuck off," Louie said through gritted teeth.

Vann remained where he was. "This mark was made on us straight after birth. Our father did it, although how he had the time and sense to do that given the…circumstances I don't know. He cut our skin with a hunting knife so we'd always know where we belonged."

"And where is that?" Louie asked, hating himself for butting in but unable to stop himself. His need to protect Jace overrode his manners.

"Crossways Compound." Vann shrugged, seemingly embarrassed by the simplicity of the cross meaning.

"Hardly an ingenious idea," Louie said, the words sour on his tongue, sour in the air too.

Stop being such a bastard.

"It's simple, I agree." Vann shrugged again.

Louie held back the need to snap out the question of whether Vann's father was simple too but knew he'd run the risk of alienating Jace. Louie wasn't usually such a testy prick, but the idea of losing Jace...

Yeah, losing your mate before you've even had him. Wise move, asshole.

Jace managed to get to his feet. Louie jumped up, ready to catch him if he fell.

"Take it steady," Louie said, holding Jace's elbow, wishing things were different, that him touching Jace while they were naked was a different scenario altogether.

Jace lifted his chin. "That mark. You could have heard about mine, heard the story of me being taken in here, and made the same cross on yourself. How do I know you're genuine? How do I know where the hell you've come from? I don't know my family, but the fact that I was abandoned on the roadside is common knowledge around here. I'm not sure I even *want* to meet my family, anyway. Not sure I want anything to do with you."

Jace turned his back on Vann, and Louie caught the look of pain on his face. Shit, Jace was hurting. The person who had brought on that hurt stood just over there. Close enough that if Louie wanted to launch himself at him, he could shove him in the pool to give himself and Jace time to get away. The thought of Vann following them to the compound, of him finding out where their safe haven was, turned him cold, though.

Sergeant had always said never to bring strangers back, to call for help instead and the pack would come.

Louie shifted to wolf so fast it clearly caught Vann off guard.

Vann took several steps back, hands raised. "Whoa. I don't want any trouble, I swear." One of his feet was so close to the edge of the pool he was in danger of slipping in.

Go on, fall.

Louie nudged Jace's leg with his snout. Jace swiveled round to stare Vann in the eyes. The expression of defeat was plain on Vann's face—that and a shade of sorrow at the fact that he'd found what he'd been searching for but hadn't been welcomed in the way he might have imagined or hoped. Open arms and tearful hugs. Twenty-five years of being apart ended in an instant as happiness at finding one another soared through them.

A pang of guilt slithered in Louie's gut, but he ignored it. No use getting sentimental. Vann could explain himself to Sergeant while Louie got Jace back to the compound.

But what if Jace doesn't want to go back with me?

To combat feelings of loss taking over him, Louie did what he'd originally intended and howled for help. He let his call go on for longer than he usually would, inserting as much urgency into the plea as he could. Jace shifted too, joining him in their distress signal. Louie was filled with a sense of companionship, of them two together against the world—a world that had turned grim on the spin of a dime, a roll of fate's dice.

"It's what I'd have done," Vann shouted above their wavering voices. "I wouldn't expect anything else. I don't belong here—I understand where you're coming from, believe me."

Vann had sounded genuine, but some people were good at that, hiding their true intent behind a friendly façade. When it came to Jace, Louie wasn't inclined to trust any fucker, cross on his chest or not.

Louie ceased his call as he heard the responding echo from several of their pack. Help would be on the way. All that was left to do was wait and keep an eye on Vann. If Louie were being honest, he didn't think Vann was a threat. Unless he counted Jace going with him. *That* was a threat all right.

A threat to Louie's sanity.

He'd go mad without Jace around, but he remembered what his mother used to say. *'If you love someone, be prepared to let them go.'*

He loved Jace—loved him to distraction—but was it so deeply that he *could* let him go? Louie wasn't naïve enough to think he could do the right thing without kicking up a fuss. When it came to saying goodbye, he wouldn't be able to hold it together. He knew that as sure as hens laid eggs. And as sure as bears shit in the woods, he'd mourn Jace until he returned.

But what if he doesn't? What if he finds someone else?

Louie shook his head, clenched his teeth, realizing he'd bared them, that he looked menacing, but he failed to give a shit.

Serves me right for keeping my feelings quiet. I deserve the loneliness—if I'd have gone all in and told him how I feel, there'd be no question of Jace leaving the compound.

But I kept it to myself because I knew this day would come and Jace needed the freedom to leave if he wanted to. I did it for him.

"Hey," Vann said, taking another step back, unfortunately away from the bank. "No need to get angry. Cover those teeth up, all right? I seriously have no beef with you. I'll wait over here until your alpha comes, yeah?"

Louie nodded, pressing himself closer to Jace.

"Fuck," Jace whispered. "What if he's for real? What the hell do I do then?" Jace hunkered down, draping an arm over Louie's back. "I have something to tell you. A secret."

Louie had no bloody clue what that might be. Probably something like Jace always feeling an outcast. That wasn't a secret. It was obvious he felt that way from his surly looks and barely polite conversations. He verged on being rude, ungrateful, but Sergeant had told everyone to tolerate him, to give him time to adjust. Someone else had muttered that twenty-five years was a long time to tolerate someone with a bad temper, and if Louie wasn't screwed up in love with Jace he'd have agreed. The thing was, Louie would take any manner of mood from Jace so long as Jace was around.

Louie whined. He hadn't meant to let it slip out, but the sound of pain had Jace gasping.

"What's up?" Jace asked. "Did you hurt yourself? I couldn't stand it if— Forget it. I didn't mean to say th— Fuck, yes I did." He leaned closer, one eye on Vann, and put his other arm across Louie's chest, holding him in their first embrace. "I fucking love you. That's my secret. I've *always* loved you, but seeing as you never really noticed me, and that I might be going with Vann to meet my family, and I may as well because you won't want me around now… Well, you won't have to be embarrassed over what I said, will you?"

Louie choked out an odd noise. He wanted to shift back so much but had to stay in wolf form in case the others called out and needed a response. Plus, much as he'd started to think Vann might be genuine, he couldn't take the man on as a human if Vann was inclined to change tack and start something. Vann was too tall, too damn big—too damn *there*.

Fuck off, Vann. Just… Just fuck off.

Jace's admission staggered Louie. He'd often envisioned such a declaration, always hoped he'd say those words but had never really thought he would. And now, when Louie wanted to say the same thing back, he couldn't. He turned his head into Jace, licked his chest then lifted his snout so he could nuzzle Jace's ear, all on the side where Vann couldn't see. Who knew if the man was a homophobe?

"Shit," Jace said quietly. "Is this what I think it is?"

Louie reared back. Nodded. Stared into Jace's eyes so he could pick up on the emotion there.

"This is so embarrassing," Jace whispered. "My cock's hard and there's him over there, and the rest of the pack will be here in a minute."

Louie tossed his head to one side, indicating the pool. Jace stood, his back to Vann, and sidled to the water. He got in, sinking so the surface was waist height. Louie chuffed out what could be classed as a wolf chuckle, hoping Jace didn't take it the wrong way. The last thing Louie wanted was Jace thinking he found his erection funny. What he'd chuckled at was Jace likely chanting at his cock for it to go down.

"You okay?" Vann asked, looking at Jace.

"Yes, thanks." Jace didn't offer a smile. He glared at Vann in his usual belligerent way.

Vann would have no idea that was Jace's normal face. Fuck, this man had so much to learn about Jace. And he *would* be learning. What Jace had said made that quite clear, that he might be going with Vann.

Might? Had he meant he'd go with Vann if Louie didn't feel the same way about Jace? Confusion warred with his need to be able to speak, but Louie consoled himself that there would be time enough for them to talk once they got back to the compound. Louie watched Vann, who gazed into the forest, obviously expecting hordes of wolves to come racing out any second.

"They're a good bunch of people," Jace said to Vann. "The wolves who took me in. Don't be rude to them. Don't treat them like shit. I've done enough of that as it is, and God, I feel bad for it. But I couldn't help myself. I didn't want them to love me, for me to love them. They weren't mine, do you understand? And I wasn't theirs. So why *would* they want to care about me?"

Vann smiled. "I love them for looking after you. For finding you in the first place. If a compound can accept an orphan and bring them up as their own—they've got to be pretty decent people."

"They are. And I probably do love them deep down—one of them I *know* I do"—he glanced at Louie—"but until you showed up, I didn't have the balls to admit it. The thought of leaving here... I see now this is my home, and I'm sick at myself for not accepting that a long time ago. I wanted my *real* home, my real family, yet all this time I had them anyway. Just that we aren't related by blood. Fuck, I've been such a dick."

Louie whined. Vann nodded.

"I see we're the same that way too," Vann said, jerking his head at Louie. "We both have strong feelings for a man."

The sudden need to sit had Louie down on his ass.

"What?" Jace asked.

"You heard me." Vann smiled again. "My mate is back there in the forest. Waiting for me. I just hope your pack don't attack him."

"They won't, they're a peaceable sort." Jace came out of the water, sans hard-on.

"Oh, I don't know. After the type of call you two just gave…" Vann shoved a hand through his hair. "They might think we're here to cause harm."

A rush of air brought the scent of other members of the pack. Louie stared from Jace to Vann to the trees on his right. Wolves stalked out, heads low, teeth sharp exhibits beneath drawn back lips.

"It's okay," Jace said, holding up one hand. "This man here. He reckons he's my brother."

Chapter Three

As Jace knew he would, Sergeant shifted. He was a monster of a man, well over seven feet, with shoulders broad enough to take on the worries of his pack. Fair-minded and generous, Sergeant hadn't deserved Jace's cantankerous attitude for the past quarter of a century, but now wasn't the right moment to apologize. That would have to wait. The clouds in Sergeant's eyes and the thunder in his loud grunt of response meant he was on the edge.

"Who are you?" Sergeant demanded.

"My name is Vann Johnson, sir, from Crossways Compound, other side of Texas. You know it?" Vann tipped his head respectfully.

He was a gentleman, it seemed.

A far cry from who I am. He puts me to shame.

"I've heard a bit." Sergeant bowed his arms by his sides. "None of it good. But why haven't I heard about them missing a cub? Why, when I put word out that I'd found one years ago, didn't someone come forward to claim him?"

"My father was unable to get a message out." Vann winced. "We were…forced to remain on the compound under strict orders from Alpha Bennett. No one was to get in, no one was to get out. Anyone found passing messages would be…" Vann cleared his throat and closed his eyes momentarily. When he opened them again, he frowned. "Would be eaten to death."

What? Eaten to death? What kind of place is Crossways for that to be allowed to happen? What kind of man is their alpha? Christ Almighty…

Sergeant kept his expression neutral. "I gather that Crossways still holds onto old beliefs and rituals, then. That kind of thing was banned over fifty years ago. Eating a pack member to death as punishment isn't something wolves should be doing these days. It's punishable by wolf law, did you know that?"

"No, sir," Vann said. "Life at Crossways is strictly governed. I don't know any laws except those our alpha tells us about."

Sergeant grunted. "So if that's the case, that no one is allowed in or out of Crossways, how come that cub was all the way over this side of Texas?"

"My parents escaped from Crossways. They didn't realize my mother was pregnant at the time." Vann closed his eyes.

Was he seeing his parents—*their* parents—in his head?

What do they look like? Do we favor our mother or father?

"Go on," Sergeant said.

"The night she had us—me and my brother there, and our sister, Terena—Mother was in the car with my father. They were frightened—they'd seen one of our pack in the town and knew time was running out. They'd be caught. The thought of that sent my mother into early labor." He shrugged. "So she gave birth in the car, my father helping as best he could then marking us, but Alpha Bennett's men pulled up. Yanked the car door open. We kids... We shifted—as you know it's a natural thing to do once born—and we were tossed out onto the verge while my parents were subjected to... Well, let's just say they were treated badly. And by the time the men told my parents to get in their truck, my brother had wandered off..."

Jace grimaced at the emotions flowing through him. He didn't know his parents, but it was as if he did. He felt their anguish, their terror, and the wrench of separation as the truck was driven away, leaving him behind. How was it possible to know this, to feel it and see it like it was a memory? Had it always been there and he'd suppressed it? Had it pained him that much he'd been unable to accept it had happened so he'd erased it from his mind? Could a cub even *have* memories from that young?

"Alpha Bennett isn't on my list of people I want to deal with," Sergeant said. "But I will have to verify what you've said. You understand that, don't you?"

Vann nodded. "I do, but if he knows I've been here, he'll lie about everything I've told you. He'll come for me. And he'll rip your compound apart while he's at it."

"He can fucking try," Sergeant said.

Several wolves barked in agreement.

"Tough man, is he?" Sergeant asked.

"He is. We've obeyed him without question for years. It was only when I heard about having a brother that we dared to escape."

"We?" Sergeant narrowed his eyes.

"My mate. He's in the forest back there. Waiting."

Sergeant glanced in that direction. "Tell him to come on out."

Vann whistled, and Jace wasn't sure he'd be okay with that if Louie called him the same way. It was demeaning, like Vann thought his mate beneath him.

"Sub, is he?" Sergeant asked.

"He is, sir." Vann smiled.

"I see." Sergeant turned to the Highgate wolves. "Back up but stay close. Just get out of a sight for a bit."

Jace was once again reminded of Sergeant's kindness, how he always put other people's feelings first. He obviously didn't want Vann's mate freaked out by too many wolves. No amount of saying sorry would fix what Jace had put Sergeant through. Jace would forever be mad at himself for behaving the way he had, basically throwing Sergeant's kindness back at him every time he'd showered Jace with it.

Fuck.

A wolf crept out of the trees, head down, subservient in more ways than just being respectful because an alpha was present. It was in every one of his movements, that need to serve, and Jace wondered what kind of man he was. In wolf form he wasn't very big—less than average for a male—and very, very white. His eyes were teal, and there was a faint glow in them, as though the animal was some kind of ethereal being. He padded toward Sergeant. He sat and bowed his head then stood so he could back up to stand beside Vann.

"I sense no bad intent from either of you," Sergeant said. "And believe me, I would. I've been an alpha for a long time, trained to spot bullshit." He scraped a palm over his chin. "What the fuck to do, eh?" Seeming to come to a decision, he said, "Louie, take

Jace back home. Stay with him in his apartment. I don't want to see either of you until the morning." He smiled. "You have *things* to sort out, right?"

Jace blushed so hard his cheeks burned. Had his love for Louie been that obvious?

Louie butted Jace's thigh, urging him toward the direction of the compound.

"What's going to happen?" Jace asked Sergeant.

"So *now* you want to know? In front of all these people? Bet you wish you'd let me tell you about mating now, don't you?" Sergeant winked. "But whatever you do, I don't think I want to know all the ins and outs of what you'll get up to, d'you catch my drift?"

Jace's cheeks flamed hotter. "No, I meant with Vann. What'll be happening there?"

Sergeant placed a hand on Jace's shoulder. "I'll do for him and his mate what I did for you. I'll take them in if that's what they want. Vann is family."

Jace had to blink pretty damn hard. "I... I shouldn't have been so... Fuck, I'm so sorry. For how I've been."

Sergeant squeezed his shoulder. "It doesn't matter. Not now you've seen the light. And that's all I've been waiting for. I knew it would come. Go on now. Your mate's impatient."

Jace swallowed, put his hand on Sergeant's, unable to say anything more. He glanced at Vann, who stood with his hand on the white wolf's head. Vann nodded, and Jace gave him the once-over again—the face so similar to his, the cross...

My brother.

Jace smiled tightly, showing emotion still so foreign to him, then shifted. Without waiting for Louie, he darted into the woods and past the other dark-furred wolves as though shame itself chased his ass brandishing a pitchfork. Louie yelped out behind him—*wait for me*, he might have said—and, once Jace had lost himself in the thickness of the trees, he came to a stop. Panting, he waited for Louie to catch up. Once they were side by side, they raced home, and for the first time in his life, despite the sorrow he'd carried for as long as he could remember, he had something positive to look forward to.

Getting to know his brother.

And Louie. Yeah, he'd be getting to know him better all right.

At last!

* * * *

Jace's apartment was small, third floor up in a block adjacent to the main compound house. Although people lived in apartments that were dotted on the grounds, everyone came together at the pack house most nights, to swap news or generally seek company. If Louie hadn't been the object of Jace's desire—and before he'd become an adult, the object of his childish affection—Jace would never have gone to those nightly get-togethers once he'd been old enough to live alone. He went there to see Louie, no other reason.

Jace had been brought up in the pack house, Sergeant and his mate, Dillon, as his surrogate parents. They'd given him all a cub could wish for— love, patience, understanding, a cuff round the earhole when he'd stepped out of line—but he'd always felt 'extra' somehow, surplus to their requirements. And he supposed he had been, although Sergeant or Dillon would never admit as much.

Jace imagined being with Louie, together as a couple, and having a cub thrust upon them, a responsibility neither might want. Jace wasn't sure he could accept a cub like that, the way Sergeant and Dillon had done with him. His arrival had been a life changer for them, and ever since then Jace had rejected all their attempts at being more than just caretakers. They'd tried to be actual parents — and Jace hadn't let them. He'd remained aloof, hoping that if he made himself invisible, they could get on with their lives as though he'd never been a part of them. The way their lives should have been. Guilt at intruding on their chosen path had always gnawed at him, and although they'd never given him any indication that they'd have preferred their relationship without him in it, he'd taken it upon himself to solve one of their problems by distancing himself and not calling on them to be his parents. It was the least he could do in return for all they'd done for him — but he hadn't been able to explain that to them. Emotion just wasn't something he could deal with very well.

He stood staring over the vast lawn at the woods, imagining Sergeant talking things out with Vann, putting down rules that had to be followed no matter what. Vann and his mate would be watched closely, and they'd no doubt stay in the main pack house until they'd earned enough trust for an apartment of their own. How was it that Sergeant could just keep on giving? Was there no end to his kindness?

The click of the kettle brought him out of his thoughts — and the sound of Louie coming into the kitchen to stand behind him. Jace shivered with anticipation, not knowing what happened in cases like this. Sergeant had tried to explain the mating ritual to him but, as usual, Jace had brushed him off, telling him he didn't need to know jack shit.

How he wished he'd listened.

"I'm kind of worried I'm going to fuck this up," Louie said.

I know exactly how you feel.

"So if I do, forgive me?" Louie rested a hand on Jace's shoulder.

Jace jumped, thinking that if he'd closed the window blinds he wouldn't be able to see the look of anxiety on Louie's face reflected in the glass.

"Will you forgive me too?" Jace asked.

"I'll forgive you anything—never forget that." Louie sighed. "Listen, I'm sorry I didn't tell you before. You know, about how I felt. But I was afraid you'd tell me to fuck right off."

"Same here." Jace laughed, the sound an unsteady wavering. "Plus I'm just an outright asshole who can't seem to express himself. It's going to be tough. You know, opening up to you. Letting you in. I'm so used to being insular that…"

"I get it. And it's okay. We'll get through this. Somehow." Louie chuckled. "We're a pair of virgins, right? We'll stumble through this together."

Louie is a virgin? Jesus. I thought… I thought when he'd been into town…

Jace had tormented himself many a night wondering whose bed Louie was warming. Whose cock he touched, whose dick was up his ass. Whose mouth he kissed. It had been torture every Friday night, watching as Louie had sped off the compound in his car then onto the main road that led to Morgan Creek, the nearest town. He frowned at that name. Morgan Creek must have been where his parents had hidden out for a time. Had they been on their way to this compound that night? Had they been prepared to beg for help? If they'd made it, Sergeant would have taken them in, no problem.

"Yeah, we'll stumble through," Jace said. "But maybe not tonight. I'm all mixed up. Got so much crap going on in my head. Like, I keep thinking of my parents. How long were they in town, you know? And would anyone remember them now, all these years later?"

"We could go and ask around tomorrow, if you want," Louie said. "Once we have a talk with Vann, find out what names they used back then. Because they'd have used fakes, surely. Old Percy in the saloon—he might remember a couple fitting their description. Percy has a memory like a fucking elephant. He can tell me what time I was last in there and what time I left, what day it was and what I was wearing. He should have been a cop."

Jace laughed quietly, although he didn't find anything remotely funny. His parents' plight gnawed at his gut, churning his stomach until he brought up a bit of acid. He caught a glimpse of movement outside and moved closer to the window, cupping his hands around his eyes so he could see into the darkness. There they were, the dark pack wolves plus two new ones, running as if they'd been together all their lives. Sergeant's charm had worked on them—Vann and his mate had had the grace to accept the offer of joining this pack.

I need to learn grace. I need to learn so many things.

He snapped the blinds closed. Turned to face Louie. Saw such love in his tawny eyes Jace was hard pressed not to break down with the enormity of his emotions. He'd gained a brother and the love of Louie in a short space of time. The reality of it crashed down on him, and he stared helplessly, not knowing how to put his feelings into words.

Instead of trying, he just said, "Hold me?" and held out his arms.

Louie embraced him, clutching him so close and tight that for a moment Jace couldn't breathe. But that was okay, he could deal with that. To have lived twenty-five years without allowing anyone to breach a certain invisible line, to finally erase that line and let someone step over… To be hugged for the first time in years, since he was a pre-teen cub… Relief washed through him, a swish of waves that frothed inside him much like the tide did on the shore. He gasped as if drowning, only to suddenly realize those gasps were sobs and tears streamed down his face.

But that was okay too. He could cry now. He was in his intended mate's arms and he had family — real and adopted.

Jace had everything a man could wish for and then some.

Chapter Four

Louie floundered. He'd hoped for this for so long that now it was here he wasn't sure what to do. It was all very well having fantasies, thinking of Jace and imagining them fucking, but to actually be in his bed, beside him?

Christ. Do I touch him? No, he said he might not want anything to happen tonight. Hold him, then? Should I do that? Offer some kind of comfort because of the shock he's had? What would I want in his shoes? A hug, I reckon.

Holding Jace had to be better than what they were doing now, resting side by side with inches of mattress between them. It reminded Louie of how they'd been throughout their lives. Always at a distance, albeit a close one, neither of them having the balls to breach the gap. It felt awkward, like they hadn't known each other their whole lives. Then again, *did* they even know each other?

No, not really.

Jace kept himself to himself, even on the nightly visits to the pack house. Louie had often wondered why Jace bothered to go there, wishing it was to see him but telling himself it wasn't. Not wanting to build his hopes up even more than he already had. Jace sat in the corner on his own more often than not, that surly expression taking over his face, a negative air hanging over him like a big old cloud. It warned people off, that unless folks wanted to get soaked in a downpour or electrocuted by lightning, it was better to stay away.

Louie had caught Jace looking at him on numerous occasions during their lives, and optimism had bloomed, a riotous patch of flowers in his gut. But the petals had quickly wilted and fallen, to dry out on the ground, crumbling to dust when they were trampled underfoot. Jace's foot. Yet Louie had continued to dream, despite knowing Jace would want to find his family one day.

Louie had never *really* contemplated that his family *would* come to find him, though. Too many years had passed with no contact, not even a word. Vann's explanation had covered that, and Louie wondered, if Alpha Bennett hadn't had such a strong hold on his pack, whether Jace would have been collected much sooner. If they'd come for him as a newborn, Louie would never have known Jace existed, and that led to another scenario. Them being fated as mates—how would they have met, living on opposite sides of Texas? Would something have happened to bring them together? Was that how things worked? That if you were meant to be with someone, destiny found a way of bringing you together? Or if you were meant to be apart, fate could also work it so that happened.

Shit. Is that why Vann is here? Has he come as fate's messenger? Are we meant to be apart? Have my feelings been something I just wished for? Are we even meant to be mated?

And now there was Vann, that messenger, a taller, wider version of Jace, someone who had the potential to rip Louie's world apart if he felt like it. But now Jace had admitted his feelings to Louie, if he mated with him, they'd never be apart. If Jace went to Crossways Compound to try to get his parents and sister released, Louie would go with him. Mates rarely went anywhere without the other, unless one was a partner to an alpha. Responsibility to the pack meant an alpha and his mate might have to spend time apart.

Louie sighed, *things* swirling round in his head, scenario after scenario. Fear played a part in every scene, throwing up question after question. What if their mating wasn't a true bond? What if they fucked and bit and scratched and they didn't gain telepathy? What if they just *thought* they were destined to be mates because there weren't many other wolves to choose from?

All those question marks were doing his head in, bobbing inside his mind.

"What are you thinking?" Louie asked to get his focus onto something else.

He turned his head to look at Jace, who was staring at the ceiling with his arms crossed over his stomach. Jace seemed closed off, and hugging himself like that... Did he need Louie to hold him in his arms instead?

"Shit you probably won't want to know," Jace said. "I keep thinking that yeah, I love you — somehow, I don't know where that came from, it's always been there — but I've been brought up with you, so maybe I just would. But then there's the fact that I've never let anyone in, never allowed myself to love anyone but you, so I *must* love you, right?" Jace laughed, the acidic type of chuckle that meant he didn't find anything funny at all. "Then I feel bad that I'm thinking about you—us—and not the huge thing that just happened in the woods. I have a brother, a family, for fuck's sake, who would have looked for me if they could have got away. I should be thinking about that before you, don't you think? Yet you're more important—so yeah, I guess I *do* fucking love you."

Although Jace was hurting, was undoubtedly confused, a glow of happiness set up home in Louie's belly. They'd sort of been thinking along the same lines, and that had to count for something, didn't it? Their primary thoughts were about each other, not the brother who had come in and upset the applecart. But had Vann really upset anything? His arrival had forced Jace to admit his feelings, and Louie would be forever grateful to him for that. If not for Vann turning up, Louie and Jace might have danced around their mate status for years to come.

"I've loved you forever," Louie said. "I remember when I first saw you, about a year after you were brought here. You'd been kept inside before that. Then one day there was this cub—clumsy little fucker—waddling across the garden, Sergeant and Dillon close behind. And my first thought was that I'd have a new playmate. I ran over, gave you a bit of a sniff, a lick, and you smacked me round the face and snarled. Remember that?"

Jace laughed—properly this time. "Yeah, I'll never forget it. I wanted to follow you everywhere after that. No idea why I hit out at you, though."

"If you think about it, all you knew was Sergeant and Dillon. I imagine they kept you inside to keep you safe. There were a few other newborns here around the time you arrived. Maybe they thought you'd be rejected or hurt by them. Maybe they loved you so much they didn't want to share."

Jace let out a pained groan. "Don't. I feel so bad for the way I've been. Too wrapped up in not belonging, making sure I *didn't* belong by behaving like a selfish prick. And all those years could have been so much happier. It's just there was something inside me, really strong, that wouldn't let me forget Sergeant and Dillon weren't my parents. I wanted a mom like everyone else—and Dillon is *so* not mom material and *so* not anyone I could have been born to."

Louie chuckled, thinking of the big black wolf—black as a human too. "He's a good man—they both are. You were lucky it was Sergeant who found you and not a full human. You'd have been taken to Lording Institute and—"

"See, that's bothering me too. How could I have been so interested in myself to have thought—and I did—that I'd have been better off at Lording than here? That I'd have had a bigger chance of being claimed? Everyone knows if you lose a wolf you check in at Lording or any of the other wolf havens. I used to imagine my parents contacting them every day, crushed when they had the news that no kid found on the roadside had been brought in. It was like I hated Sergeant for denying me that, you know?"

Louie couldn't imagine what had been going through Jace's head over the years and he was surprised Jace wasn't a fuck-up. That he wasn't was all down to Sergeant and Dillon. They'd reminded Jace time and again that he was loved, welcomed, and part of the pack family—no matter where he'd originated. Louie had watched the two older wolves struggling to get through to Jace, and Louie had wanted to join them, to bring about the light-bulb moment where Jace finally understood that family didn't necessarily have anything to do with blood. Still, that light-bulb moment was here now, and Jace would have a truckload of guilt to deal with in the future.

"I'll be here for you," Louie said. "To help you get through this. For a start, stop beating yourself up. What's done is done. The past can't be changed but the future can. From here on out, be who you really are. Not some angry man who's only angry because it hides your true personality. Be Jace, the man you were always meant to be. The man I know is inside."

Jace reached out and took Louie's hand. The warmth from their skin touching sent shivers through Louie, and although he wanted to turn onto his side and press his body flush with Jace's, although he wanted to kiss him, he decided not to push it. There was time enough for them to explore one another. More important things had to be sorted out first.

"I'll wait for however long it takes. You know, us mating," Louie said. "I don't know what I'm doing, how to do it. How to even kiss, for fuck's sake."

"Me neither, but I've dreamt about it. Christ, have I dreamt about it." Jace squeezed Louie's hand. "And much as Vann turning up freaked me out—I mean, who faints over something like that?—he's not so important. My parents and sister aren't so important. I don't know them, but I know you and Sergeant and Dillon. I think what's happened is, although I spent my life pushing my pack family away, Vann coming made me realize that I'd longed for my real family when I had a damn good one here all along." He sighed. "I'll maybe meet with my mom, dad and sister one day—and I feel so damn sorry for them trapped at

Crossways—but my life is here, always has been, always will be."

Louie couldn't stop his grin of relief. "Shit, you have no idea how happy I am to hear you say that. But aren't you curious, even just a bit? Aren't you worried about your blood relations?"

"I am, but no more worried than I would be if anyone else was held against their will. There's no bond with them, no link of love, so how can I truly worry? Make sense? It makes me sound a bastard but..." He shook his head. "Anyway, Sergeant will sort it. He'll find them, get them out, bring them back here—or wherever they want to go. He'll make sure they're safe. Sergeant's one hell of a man, I see that now. Everything will turn out okay, I know it." He paused. "So, will you kiss me?"

Louie's stomach rolled. Fuck, *that* moment was here. What if he messed it up? What if he slobbered all over him, or his tongue didn't work properly? What if...?

"Yeah," Louie said. "I can give it a go."

And that was about all he *could* do—give it a go. It'd be trial and error for both of them, he had to remember that. If Jace had fucked and kissed before, Louie would feel a damn sight more awkward, more of a novice. But it was an even playing field—they'd opened the book on the same page. All right, it was a blank page, but if they both wrote on it quickly, filled it up, if they made mistakes, they could turn that one and write some more on a fresh sheet.

Louie swallowed down his nerves and turned onto his side. Jace did the same, and they stared at one another for what seemed the longest time. Was Jace thinking along the same lines as Louie? That fuck, here they were at last, on a bed, together. Close—so close Jace's hot breath fanned Louie's face. So close that if Louie just moved forward a bit their lips would meet.

Jace was the one to make that move. His lips pressed to Louie's, soft, gentle, and Louie's cock grew so hard it hurt. Twenty-five years old and a damn virgin. Twenty-five years of wondering what a kiss would be like. And here it was, driving him to inch closer to Jace, as though it was the most natural thing in the world. And it was, wasn't it? Being with a mate had to be one of the best things in life. And yeah, this *was* the best. Although their lips just about brushed, Louie would remember this as the best kiss of his life.

He closed his eyes and thought about opening his mouth but wasn't sure what the hell to do after that. Again, Jace took the lead, slipping the tip of his tongue out and tracing the seam. The contact sent a bolt of lust to Louie's cock and, breathless, he knew he'd have the embarrassment of coming quickly to contend with. Jace would be the same, wouldn't he? This was something they should have experienced in their late teens when the excuse of youth could be used as a way of explaining fast ejaculation. A grown man having to mutter reasons why he'd come in his pants without his cock even being touched...? If that happened, he just hoped Jace would understand.

Jace parted Louie's lips with his tongue. Louie held his breath while he waited to see what would happen next. They were still holding hands, and Louie gripped hard, his innocence preventing him from letting go to explore other parts of Jace's body. This was the real deal, really fucking happening, and he told himself to just let everything unfold and for him to do what felt natural and right.

So Louie slid *his* tongue out, gliding it over Jace's, the sensations producing a rush of tingles all over his body. He moaned, a flush flooding his face because he hadn't meant to make a sound, and clutched Jace's hand harder. His balls ached, his cock strained against his jeans, and by God, he was just about going to come already.

"This… I'm going…" he whispered.

"Me too. It's… Everything's so exciting."

Louie opened his eyes to find Jace looking at him. His stomach rolled. He'd been caught peeking, but then his cock twitched so sharply his hips bucked, shoving his cock into Jace's. Primal need took over, and Louie reached over and touched Jace's ass. He pressed him as close as he could get him, and the rock-solidness of Jace's dick had Louie grinding against it. The movement gave enough friction, enough simulation of jerking off or fucking, that Louie's cum swirled in the root of his cock.

"Oh, shit," he panted. "I'm really going to—"

Jace snuffed out the words with a kiss. It involved a messy, uneducated tongue that went every which way. Louie went with it, kissing him back, rutting against Jace as Jace did the same to him. A frantic press of cock to cock, a feverish dance of mouth to mouth. It was hot, new and so fucking electrifying. Heat filled Louie—on his skin and inside his balls and cock. He cried out into Jace's mouth, digging his fingertips into Jace's ass to hold him steady. Jace shoved his fingers into Louie's hair while Louie cack-handedly slid his free arm under Jace's side to put his hand to Jace's back, fingers splayed. Locked together, they imitated a penetrative fuck, just grinding against one another, the newness of what was happening overwhelming Louie.

He came—Jesus Christ, he came. Hard. Hot. His body jerking out of time with Jace's. He kissed on, desperate to keep the intense pleasure going, and when Jace bucked and groaned hoarsely, another series of cum spurts flooded Louie's underwear. His heart pattered way too fast, his lungs filled with trapped air, but he rutted on, never wanting his orgasm to end.

This. This was what he'd been waiting for.

And fuck, it had been well worth the wait.

Chapter Five

Jace woke to sunlight streaming through the window directly into his eyes. He blinked, wondering why he hadn't closed the curtains. Then he remembered. He and Louie had gotten on the bed last night, emotionally exhausted. But it hadn't stopped them... Jesus, they had fucked. Well, kissed and messed about, but it had felt like proper fucking.

As though his memories had awakened sensations, he winced as the hard material of his jeans grazed his cock. They'd fallen asleep without cleaning up. Jace hadn't wanted to break the spell, and it had seemed that Louie hadn't either. They'd stayed close in an embrace, talking and talking until... Who had fallen asleep first? Jace couldn't recall, but he did know he'd drifted off peacefully, the first time ever without worries or angst plaguing his mind. And that was weird, wasn't it? His life was more complicated now than it had ever been. By rights he should have had insomnia, all the worries in his world gatecrashing his mind, making sure he couldn't rest.

He glanced at Louie, who slept on. The man's lips were parted, and soft puffs of air escaped. His eyelids fluttered, and Jace wondered what he was dreaming about. Him? He eyed Louie's groin. Sex? His dick was certainly bulging his jeans. If Jace had the courage he'd get that cock out, set it free to hold it in his palm. But this kind of stuff was so new to him, and although he'd been bold enough to push for more than just hugs last night, in the cold light of day…

So much had happened so fast. Yesterday he'd been pining, as usual, hoping for this, then suddenly Vann had appeared, giving Jace exactly what he wanted with Louie. If he had something to thank Vann for, that was it. As for coming into his life, announcing that Jace had a brother, a sister, a mother and a father… He wasn't sure he wanted to thank him for that. And wasn't that just ironic? All his life Jace had mourned the family he'd never known, and now their existence had come to light, served up to him on a plate, he realized he wasn't all that hungry after all.

Annoyed by the constant thoughts raging through his head, wanting a bit of peace where he could just be free of hassle for a few moments, he got out of bed, careful not to wake Louie. In the bathroom he stripped then hopped in the shower. Clean and refreshed, he went back to the bedroom to dress. Louie was awake, hair mussed, a shit-eating grin filling his face.

"Morning," Louie said. "D'you know, I never thought I'd wake up here."

Jace smiled. "I always wished you would, but I know what you mean. Never really thought it would happen. Didn't think I'd get that lucky."

"Same." Louie smiled back. "You okay?"

"Yeah, you?"

"More than. Can I use your shower?"

Jace nodded. "What's yours is mine, man." It felt good to say that.

As Louie passed him, he brushed his fingers down Jace's arm. This was the stuff of Jace's fantasies, the pair of them together like this. He wanted to pinch himself, make sure this wasn't one of his millions of dreams.

"Can't believe you're here," Jace said once contact was severed and Louie was almost at the bathroom door.

"Me neither, but I am, and fuck, it's good, isn't it?"

"Too good." Jace turned to see Louie stripping. He should have felt like a pervert, a twisted voyeur for watching him shed his clothes, but he didn't. It was right, being here, staring, appreciating. "Nice ass," he blurted then flushed.

Louie didn't turn around. He stiffened his spine. "Shit, I thought you'd gone."

"Nope, still here, admiring the view. That make you uncomfortable? I mean, it's not like I haven't seen you naked before." *If the situation were reversed, how would I feel? Isn't this different from when we shift? More private?* "I'll go, give you time to yourself. Sorry, I should have thought, but you went straight in and undressed and I— I'll go."

"Don't." Louie glanced over his shoulder. "We can't keep letting embarrassment win. Shit, come in here and talk to me while I shower." He paused, sighing, as if coming to a decision. "You've seen it all before anyway… Watch me, if you like."

Did Jace like? Fuck, yeah, but could he keep away from Louie, keep distance between them when all he wanted to do was go into that bathroom and touch his skin, turn him around and get a glimpse of his cock?

Louie stepped into the shower, the curtain hiding him from view. If Jace wanted to see, he had no choice but to go in there and peer around the curtain. After taking a fortifying breath, in he went, his demeanor showing more boldness than he felt inside. The change in the sound of splashing water told him Louie was maybe in there with his hands on his head, water channeling down his arms, dripping off his elbows in a stream then hitting the tub. The soft *thwump* of lather slapping the tiles... He was washing his hair?

Leaning against the wall at the end of the tub, Jace peeked around the curtain. He had a front view of Louie this time, and Christ, what a view it was. His cock was semi-hard—and trust Jace for spying that first, but it was something he'd wanted to see in forever—and jutted from his body slightly. It was heavy-looking, not short or long, not thick or thin. Just right, Jace thought, and something he could maybe handle when the time came for it to slide into his ass.

His dick fluttered at his thoughts then went into full hard-on mode. Louie had his eyes closed as he massaged his head, and some of the shampoo froth was sliding down his forehead, heading for his eye. Jace instinctually wanted to reach into Louie's personal space to flick the froth away but remained where he was, spellbound, amazed that Louie—the man he'd wanted for too long—was actually there in his shower.

It was surreal.

His chest tightened with emotion. Everything would be all right now, wouldn't it? Having Louie here was like Jace had finally found himself, like he would be comfortable in his skin from now on. He smiled then laughed at his good fortune.

Louie tilted his head under the spray, sluicing off the lather. "My dick makes you laugh?"

"No," Jace said quickly. "I wasn't laughing about that. I'm laughing because everything's so fucking perfect." *Not everything. Just the stuff between me and you.*

"It is?"

"Yeah. Even more so if you'd show me how you jerk off." *God, did I really say that?* He hadn't intended to, but it seemed his brain and mouth were independent of him, in collusion, taking matters into their own hands no matter what Jace thought.

Louie's cock spasmed. Shot out to full hardness. He took hold of himself, curling his hand around it tentatively, as if unsure whether he ought to do as Jace had suggested. Was he as unsure as Jace?

"That's it," Jace encouraged. "Just pretend I'm not here."

Jace knew he was expecting a lot. If he were in Louie's place, he wasn't sure he'd have the guts to do anything but turn his back and hope Louie went away, at the same time wishing he'd stay.

Louie kept his eyes closed and, much to Jace's delight, set up a slow rhythm at first. Jace stared in wonder. Louie eased his hand down. His cockhead emerged from his grip, the foreskin pulled back so hard the shape of him was very clear. Jace had stared at his own cock in the past as he'd jerked off, but seeing someone else doing it brought a whole new level of *Shit, that's hot.*

"You ever played with your ass?" Jace asked, stunned that he'd done so. A violent blush came, the prickly heat jabbing at his cheeks. "I didn't mean to say that. It's just... I want to know everything about you. I don't even have time to think these things. They just come out."

"Ah, shit, the things you say..." Louie jerked on. "Yeah, I've played with my ass."

"You like it?" Jace enjoyed the feel of his fingers inside him when he stretched his hole, and the slickness of the lube enhancing his excitement.

"Yeah, I like it. Oh, God..."

"You want a cock up there?" *Jesus H, shut your damn mouth, will you?*

"You're killing me here. I didn't expect... Shit, I don't know *what* I expected, but this? You saying stuff like that? I'm going to come, man."

"You want me to catch your cum?" Jace rounded his eyes. What the hell was the matter with him? Why had words from his fantasies decided to make themselves heard here? He'd only just got together with Louie, and there he was, talking like a seasoned pro in the sex department. Did it matter? Shouldn't he just go with whatever, trusting his instincts?

"Jace, seriously, I'm going to come."

Jace went down on his knees, leaning over the edge of the tub. Some of the shower spray soaked his head, ran down his face. "Open your eyes," he said, looking up at Louie. "Come on me."

Jace almost shook his head at himself but stopped. If he had to repress who he really was with Louie, then they shouldn't be together. And Louie had told him to be who he really was...

Louie opened his eyes, his cheeks sporting a blush so red that Jace felt for him.

"It's okay, right?" Jace asked. "You're okay?"

"Yeah, but you, like this... It's more than I imagined." He gave his cock a harder set of jerks and thrust his hips toward Jace.

"You don't have to imagine anymore. Do it. Come on me."

Jace watched in fascination as Louie's body seemed to ripple. His balls drew up, the skin puckering into ridges, and the vein in his cock pulsed. Louie pointed his dick at Jace, level with Jace's mouth.

Jace parted his lips.

"Oh… Jace, I'm coming…"

Jace tipped his head forward, bold now, and closed his lips over the tip of Louie's dick. The skin was soft — *so* soft — on his tongue, and he waited for what it would churn out. Water trickled down his neck, snaked beneath his clothes. Hot — but not as hot as the cum that shot into his mouth. He shut off his throat, determined not to gag, and let each burst of spunk flood his tongue. His own dick pulsed, and before he'd had a second to process it, he came in his pants again. Louie gasped, hard and raspy, and Jace quickly swallowed, moaning while Louie pushed more of his length inside. Jace was conscious of not clamping his jaw shut as his orgasm ripped through him. He sucked that cock in so his lips covered his teeth. He grunted, rutting air, reaching down to rub his cock through his jeans.

Louie stopped coming and eased out of Jace's mouth. Jace looked up at him. Louie smiled, shaking his head a bit.

"You… We… We're good, aren't we?" Louie asked.

"Oh yeah, we're good. Except I came in my damn pants again."

Louie washed himself as Jace got to his feet. He undressed facing Louie, unsure as hell about what Louie would think of his body. But if Louie had managed to stand there naked and jerking off, Jace could do the same — minus the jerking off. His dick was so sensitive he didn't think he'd manage to come again so soon. With his clothes discarded in a heap on the floor, Jace lifted his head to stare at Louie. His stare was returned, eye contact intense until Louie lowered his gaze down Jace's body. Would Louie like what he saw? Crushed by insecurity, Jace closed his eyes, praying he was everything Louie wanted in a mate.

"You're perfect," Louie said.

Oh, thank Christ...

"I am?" He opened his eyes, seeing nothing but sincerity in Louie's.

"Fuck, yeah. Perfect. You coming in?" Louie held out a hand.

"Yeah, but there's not enough room for us to both get under the spray."

"Not a problem. I'll sit on the edge. Or wash you — if you want?"

Jace climbed in. Their bodies brushed when they switched places, the thrill of it almost too much for Jace to handle. He let the spray blast down on him. Louie poured shower gel into his palm then touched him, hand flat to Jace's chest. Jace closed his eyes and jolted with awareness that they were being intimate, that all those nights he'd spent dreaming had done nothing to prepare him for the reality.

Reality was so much sharper.

Louie washed him, soothing strokes down his belly. The lather was as soft as his touch, and as Louie ghosted his hand over Jace's cock, he was careful to wash him gently. The desire to get hard was there for Jace, but his dick wasn't playing. Not that it mattered. Just being here like this, having his body soaped by the man he loved — hell, there was nothing better.

"This is good, isn't it?" Louie asked.

"Yeah." *Should I offer to wash him, even though he's done it himself already?*

"It's like I'm exploring," Louie said, snatching Jace's thought away. "Like I'm feeling you, getting to know your shape by touch and not just by my eyes. I *know* your body already because I've studied it so much. But being able to *feel* it?"

"Yeah, I know what you mean."

All those years I thought he wasn't interested, yet he's been studying me. We've wasted a lot of time, not admitting to one another how we feel. But we'll make up for it now.

"And it's a beautiful shape," Louie went on. "Always thought so. I used to look at you and wonder what it would be like to touch you this way, and now I know. It's better than I imagined."

"*Everything's* better than I imagined. Every goddamned thing." And it was true. No amount of dreaming or imagining could measure up to this, the real deal.

Jace allowed Louie to do his thing. Skating fingers, the brushing of palms over skin, the touch of lips on his nipple… And *that* had him jerking in surprise. Who would have thought he'd like that? Louie circled his tongue around it, creating a well of lust to streak through Jace. Louie lifted his head, kissed Jace on the mouth. Jace gave in to it, went with his need to explore. He touched Louie in return. A glut of excitement squirmed in his belly that God, he was touching Louie—*touching him*.

"I could stay here forever," Louie said between kisses.

"Me too. All damn day. Yeah, like you said, forever."

It wasn't forever, just until the water turned cold, but it seemed an eternity.

A wonderful, delicious eternity.

Chapter Six

Eating breakfast at the pack house wasn't something Louie did often but he did this morning. It wasn't served early enough for him—he had to get up every weekday morning at six a.m. He enjoyed his job as clerk in the only bank in Morgan Creek but needing a run before leaving for the town meant he was a habitual early riser. Oddly, this morning that need for a run wasn't present. He supposed it was because he didn't have any angst to shake off—angst that he wanted Jace but couldn't have him.

Today being Saturday, the pack house dining room was pretty full. Folks not wanting to cook, taking the opportunity to have a break from the norm, he reckoned. He couldn't imagine living anywhere else, but he would if it meant going with Jace. Crossways wasn't somewhere Louie would ever choose to live, though. By the sound of the place it was messed up and was shrouded in the aura of times gone by, where wolf shifters were unruly and lived by dark rules that had no place in today's society. He wondered how it had affected Vann. He'd seemed polite, a gentleman.

How was that possible when his surroundings and the things his alpha must have taught them were so barbaric? Eating a pack member to death? What the fuck was all that about?

Maybe Vann's parents had a stronger influence.

Louie was just glad he'd been raised at Highgate, with morals and the knowledge that even though not everyone here was related, they might as well be. Family, that's what they all were, regardless of the blood that ran through their veins.

Crossways sounds nuts.

Louie and Jace sat at a table near the back, getting glances from other shifters.

"Guess they're wondering how come we're sitting together," Jace said. "How come we're even in here at all of a morning. I don't usually have breakfast here because I know you don't bother."

That information glowed warmly inside Louie. "Maybe word's got out. You know, about Vann. And maybe us?" He didn't feel under the microscope—much. He was proud that he could announce to the pack—albeit via actions and not words—that Jace was his mate, or at least that they'd finally breached the gap that had stretched between them throughout their lives.

"I wonder how Vann and his mate got through the night. I mean, whether they slept or stayed awake worrying. That Alpha Bennett sounds a right bastard. Vann must be worrying he'll come here, drag him back to Crossways, and sentence him to being eaten alive. Shit, I can't get over that. I'd heard wolves used to act differently back then, but to still be doing it when it's against the law? Wow." Jace ate some scrambled egg.

"We'll find out soon enough how Vann's coping. He's here now."

Sergeant and Dillon came in, Vann and another man behind them. The two latter were dressed—Sergeant must have found them some clothes. They all carried trays of food, and Sergeant looked around, probably hoping for a table where he could eat with Dillon and their new guests. Everywhere was full except for the table Louie and Jace occupied, so Louie lifted his hand to welcome them across.

Sergeant and Dillon ambled over. They sat with ease, like everything was normal, as though Louie and Jace had been a couple for years. Their behavior was nothing new. They tended to accept things easily. Vann and his mate weren't so relaxed, though. They stood behind the two remaining empty chairs, Vann glancing at Sergeant, his mate staring at the floor.

"What are you standing there for?" Sergeant asked, frowning.

"Uh…" Vann cleared his throat. "We… Alpha Bennett makes us wait until he says we can sit."

"Well, I ain't Alpha fucking Bennett. I'm Sergeant, and you sit down when you goddamn please. Otherwise your food'll get cold." He scowled. "I told you last night, you're free here. To walk around, to eat in the pack house. To join us here at night. To get jobs in Morgan Creek when the time's right—or if you want to hide out until we know the coast is definitely clear, there's plenty of work to be done on pack land." He jabbed a fork toward the empty seats. "So sit your asses down. Eat. Enjoy your freedom. Start learning to live instead of just surviving, understand?"

"Yes, sir. Thank you." Vann pulled out his chair then sat.

His mate remained where he was.

"Though the same doesn't apply to Kip there—not when you're around anyway, Vann," Sergeant said, smiling. He turned to Louie and Jace. "You need to understand that Kip'll only do stuff when Vann says so. It's a lifestyle choice, so don't go thinking Vann's an asshole, right?"

Louie nodded. He'd heard about that kind of thing—of course he had—but it wasn't something he'd ever wanted. And besides, it was none of his business what other people got up to, so long as they didn't thrust it in his face and try to get him to act the same way.

"Sit now," Vann said, giving Kip a smile.

Kip obeyed.

"And eat," Vann added.

"And while we're at it," Sergeant said, "none of this 'sir' business. I'm just Sergeant, got it?"

Vann and Kip nodded.

While everyone else tucked in, Louie studied Kip, but not overtly. He didn't want the man to be spooked by his scrutiny. Kip's hair was as white as his fur had been, his eyes the same teal as last night's wolf but without the glow. His frame, although wiry, was packed with muscle, and he reminded Louie of a kickboxer or someone like that. A sportsman. He was a stark contrast to Vann—they couldn't be more opposite—yet at the same time they were suited.

Jace squeezed Louie's thigh under the table. Louie glanced his way, hoping to read what was wrong. He wished they'd mated properly so they could share thoughts—Jace's expression was one of *I feel awkward*. Probably at being with a brother he didn't know. Being in Sergeant's and Dillon's presence. Knowing his brother was a Dom. Thinking nothing had been said for a while and he had the urge to fill the silence.

"So," Sergeant said, solving one of the problems, "there will be a meeting soon. We have a plan of action — me and Dillon stayed up most of the night working some shit out. But the basics are that we'll be sending a few wolves to Crossways Compound to scout the area, see if we can storm it. Vann and Jace's family need rescuing — they *want* rescuing so Vann says — and any other shifter who wants setting free can seek help at the various institutes until they find other compounds to take them in."

Jace squeezed Louie's leg harder.

"Who'll be going?" Jace asked.

"Not you, that's for sure. I want you kept safe," Sergeant said. "And not Vann either. You two are targets, Kip too. If Alpha Bennett gets wind of you being alive and well, Jace — you're fucked, yeah?" He paused. "And then I'm fucked. Dillon's fucked. Not having you around..." He swallowed. "Not a goddamned option for us, you hear?"

For once Jace didn't frown or give a grumpy protest. Instead, he nodded, smiled, like he was comfortable knowing that not only was Sergeant looking out for him, but that their alpha may well not want to risk Jace being harmed. He was his son in every respect but biological, after all.

"When will the scouts leave?" Louie asked.

"This afternoon," Sergeant said. "Flight to Crossways. Be there by tonight. Easier to scope it in the dark. You know how it goes."

Louie did. He'd done his fair share of patrol stints around the compound — they all had. Everyone pulled together here to keep the place safe. Full humans — fulls — knew shifters existed — that this compound was nothing *but* shifters — and for the most part they all got along. Patrolling was a daily and nightly occurrence, just in case a rogue full harbored hate and decided to take potshots at the shifters—but that hadn't happened in a long time. Not since Louie had been a kid.

"Right," Louie said. "And after that?"

Sergeant took a deep breath. Released it. "Let's say we manage to get some of our own in the compound. The idea is to keep Alpha Bennett occupied while the others are rescued. He's going to sense something's up for sure, but if he gets testy, we'll have no choice but to subdue him. Yeah, it isn't something I like doing, but with so many shifters held hostage there—and there are about ninety wolves—we can't allow this to go on any longer. I have the go-ahead from Alpha Newart, so it's not like I'm doing anything underhand."

Alpha Newart. Fuck, the head honcho himself.

"Christ," Louie said. "Will Alpha Newart be taking responsibility for Bennett?" *What a stupid question. Of course he will. He's our overall governor.*

"Yeah." Sergeant nodded as if for emphasis. "He'll be taken to Knightly Institute—as you know, that's where Newart's based. He'll be given a fair trial, but with the amount of witnesses, and news that he allows wolves to be eaten... Doesn't look good for him getting a non-guilty verdict." He shrugged. "Things'll work out."

Louie needed to get out. The room was suddenly stifling, the people closing in on him—maybe he *did* need a run. He couldn't work out why his blood had gone cold. Was it Sergeant's shrug, his nonchalance, his obvious belief that *'things'll work out'*? What if it didn't? What if it all went wrong and Bennett got away?

Fuck. He'll come looking for Vann and Kip. For Jace.

"What time is the meeting?" Louie tried to keep the strain from showing on his face.

"Midday," Sergeant said. "So if you want a run or some downtime, go ahead, although I wouldn't recommend it on a full stomach."

"I didn't eat much." And he hadn't. A few forkfuls of egg, half a sausage.

He rose, pleased that Jace did the same. They returned their trays to the serving hatch in the foyer outside the dining room then escaped onto the porch. The air had a nice nip to it, enough to blow any cobwebs away. Louie felt better for it, less hemmed in, and he took Jace's hand to lead him off the porch and onto the grass.

"Want to run?" he asked.

"Yeah, for a bit."

Jace undressed without preamble, just as if they were back to being how they'd been before. Louie would follow suit—they'd gotten naked so many times before, why should it feel different now? They weren't being sexual, that's why—and that made a huge difference. Instead of getting his kit off, Louie did what he always did and studied Jace's body. The clean-cut lines. The smooth skin that was tight over bone and muscle. The long legs. Those slender fingers of his.

The thought of those fingers entering his ass had him sucking in a breath and chanting a mundane rhyme so he didn't get hard.

It didn't work like it always had in the past.

Jace pushed his clothes into one of the clothes bins. Louie shook himself out of his voyeurism and struggled free of his clothes, anxious that he was behind in the stripping stakes, knowing that Jace could watch *him* now. It hadn't seemed a problem before his cock had decided to play up on him. But, with Louie sporting wicked wood, the normal act of disrobing before a shift had turned into an intimate encounter. For him, anyway.

Jace stared at Louie's cock as Louie dropped his jeans and boxers.

"Holy fuck!" Jace glanced around. "You're lucky no one's about, but if I were you I'd keep my ass to the windows. You don't know who might be looking out."

Louie felt better for that and laughed. "It's your fault. I saw you naked and — Christ. *You* ought to turn your ass to the windows too."

Jace glanced down at himself then swiftly turned. "We're a pair, aren't we?"

"Seems so." Naked, Louie sidled over to a clothes bin and shoved his things inside. "Better shift — that's good for deflating cocks."

"You know that from experience?" Jace asked over his shoulder, eyebrows raised.

"Too many times to count, although I made sure you never saw me with a hard-on."

Jace shifted, quick and seamless. He faced Louie. Jace bounded forward, headbutted Louie's leg then gallivanted off toward the oaks. Louie shifted. He gave chase, euphoria speeding through him that he was finally getting to run with Jace as partners. Before, there had been no playing — not after that first cuff and growl all those years ago — just running for exercise, nothing more.

Past the oaks and into the woods Jace went, Louie close behind. He chased him between the trunks, his tongue lolling from the side of his mouth, breaths faint gray clouds. It was so different out here in the daytime, more exposed despite the woods being enclosed and rife with trees. A weak sun tried valiantly to break through the clouds and leaf cover but failed, offering nothing but murky light that gave the day an autumn air.

Jace yipped, and Louie didn't suppress the swamp of enthusiasm that undulated in his belly. This was what it was all about, roaming with his mate, having fun. Running had felt good before once the apprehension left his body, but this was even better. He was freer now, lighter on his feet, and so goddamn happy.

Jace reached the pool well before Louie. He lapped at the water, and Louie would have ribbed him had they been in human form, yanking his chain that he was unfit if he needed a drink so bad already. Louie joined him, only needing his tongue wetting, then flopped down on the bank. He was out of breath himself, excited and content for the first time in what felt like forever. Jace collapsed too, panting, and, Louie would swear, smiling.

We can talk like this soon, in our heads. You'll be able to hear me, to know how I feel just by tuning in. We'd never have to speak out loud again if we didn't want to.

Louie couldn't wait for that.

Chapter Seven

The snap of a twig breaking had Jace and Louie bolting to their feet. Jace edged closer to Louie, wanting to shield him while he scented the air and peered into the surrounding foliage. Fuck, he was glad to be in wolf form. A faint whiff of *someone other* drifted toward him, and Jace's hackles rose. He growled, low and long, the sound meshing with Louie's warning.

Who the fuck's there?

His first thought was that a full had wandered onto the compound, even though there were strict rules in place that fulls left shifters alone and vice versa. Long ago, so Jace had heard by listening to Sergeant and Dillon talking as he'd grown up, wolves and fulls had gotten together to lay down regulations and create laws that protected everyone from each other. But that scent... The smell of wolf as well as human invaded his nostrils via a sharp breeze that rattled the leaves, drowning out any footsteps if the intruder were walking closer.

Shit. Damn it.

He growled louder, contemplating sending out a distress call, but until he knew exactly what they were dealing with he reckoned it was best he waited. Maybe a full was with a wolf. Maybe they were friends and had wandered onto Highgate land by accident. They might not be from around here to know this was private property. Whatever excuse Jace may come up with didn't change the fact that someone unknown had arrived at Highgate.

"No sense in growling, wolf," a man shouted, his accent thick Texan.

That voice seemed to have come from where Vann had appeared the night before. And the man didn't sound friendly. Didn't sound like someone who had just 'wandered' here. If Jace had thought this could be resolved by simply asking the man to identify himself, he knew he was sorely mistaken. An angry visitor wasn't something he'd ever had to deal with. Sergeant or Dillon had never been far away, and usually dealt with things like this—not that Jace could remember strangers being caught on the property before.

Unless Sergeant and Dillon shielded me from it.

"I got me a gun, wolf, and it's trained right on one of you," the man said.

Christ Almighty…

Jace's instincts screamed for him to run. Until now, he hadn't realized how sheltered his life had been. Guns and violence weren't a common theme at Highgate. He'd had nothing to fear all his life.

Louie darted in front of Jace, but Jace switched their places instantly. There wasn't time for a protective pissing contest, and he gave Louie the kind of growl where he'd hopefully understand what Jace meant—*Stop messing around, remain alert*. He nudged Louie with his ass, his way of saying *Back up*. On the left-hand side of the pond, high reeds swayed in the breeze. If he and Louie could just get there, they'd be somewhat shielded, especially if they hunkered down.

Slowly, they backed away—so slowly Jace hoped their movements wouldn't be noticed at first. Jace remained just in front of Louie, but to the side so he could fling himself across the second he heard a gun go off.

I should have called for help. I'm sorry, Louie, so sorry.

They managed to reverse about two meters before Jace heard another cracking twig then the man cursing. Whipping his head around to look at Louie, Jace prayed that his mate would know his intentions. He jerked his head, further expressing his plan—the same way Sergeant had taught them.

Run that way.

They turned as one, speeding for the reeds. The sound of gunfire echoed a millisecond before the bullet hit the ground in front of them, burrowing into the grass and kicking up nodules of mud. They ran faster, making it to the reeds as a second shot was fired.

Jace almost lost his breakfast.

Who the hell is that? Some kind of shifter who hunts shifters?

Whoever it was, he must have thought as a wolf he didn't stand a chance against two others. Otherwise, why the gun? The man clearly wasn't confident of his fighting ability—or maybe he was lazy and preferred trying to take them out the human way.

Behind the reeds, Jace and Louie lay as flat as possible. The thickness and density of the stems were more than adequate cover—unless someone else came at them from behind. Jace sniffed. Thankfully, the breeze that soughed through every few seconds allowed him to pinpoint exactly where their attacker was—and that there was only one man and no separate wolf.

Louie howled out a distress signal filled with terror and panic. It was clear Jace and Louie were scared going by the sound of it, but that didn't matter. Jace understood—he felt the same way—but he couldn't indulge in fear now, even though it was doing a good job in trying to take over him. He concentrated on the view ahead, scouring the trees opposite for any signs of movement.

The clouds chose that moment to set the sun free, and a shaft of light beamed down to illuminate the woods opposite. It glinted off something—the gun's sight lens?—and gave away the man's true position. With the sun blaring at the intruder, Jace moved backwards, scraping his belly over the grass. Louie made to follow, but Jace growled quietly, warning him to stay the fuck where he was.

Quickly turning, keeping close to the ground, Jace fled into the woods before Louie could stop him. He took a sharp right, which, if he followed the circle of the tree line around the pool, would take him to where he needed to be. His paws thudded on mulchy ground, and he attuned his ears to his surroundings. He glanced through trunks. Jace was pleased to see luck and the sun were on his side. The sun blasted such a strong, wide beam that hopefully the stranger would be momentarily blinded.

Louie howled out another call, longer, more panicked. The response came, quite close it seemed, as though others were out on a run and were only moments away. Confident that help would be with them any second, Jace blundered through the forest, slowing at an estimated few feet away. He couldn't see what he needed to spot until light bounced off that lens again. The man stood side-on to Jace, staring across at where Louie was, his gun well seated beneath his armpit.

Good, he doesn't know I'm here. Yet. He isn't concentrating properly. He should have heard me coming. Smelled me.

Jace crept closer, checking out the ground ahead for any rogue twigs. He didn't need to step on one now, not when he was so near to taking down his target.

Another call came from the back-up wolves.

"Goddamn motherfuckers," the man muttered, swiping at his brow with the back of one hand. He shifted the gun more securely beneath his armpit then tightened his finger on the trigger.

Jace leaped, crashing into his side. The gun went off—fuck knew where the bullet went—and the momentum of Jace's shove sent the guy face first onto the ground. Jace landed on top of him, opening his mouth intending to go straight for the jugular.

The man laughed, stopping Jace mid-action.

"What, you think by killing me this will be over, wolf? My people know where I am, and they're loyal to me, tracking me all the way. They'll come here and find you—find all of you." He sniffed. "And this'll be the right place, won't it? You got the stink of the others on you. Fucking Johnson family—you're one of them, aren't you? The missing runt."

Jace changed his original objective and bit the bastard's gun hand, shaking it while his victim screamed in pain, dropping the rifle onto a layer of leaves. The guy yanked the scruff of Jace's neck, but Jace held on, perking his ears at the sound of paws beating the ground. Louie appeared, leaping beside Jace and clamping the man's other hand between his teeth. More wolves arrived, forming a circle, snarls and snaps warning their quarry that he'd better calm the hell down now or he'd be mauled into submission.

And Jace would be the one to do it too, no question.

"Enough," Sergeant said, coming up behind Jace and Louie. "You did good, but you could go too far. Now back off. And you," he said to Jace's prey, "should stay where you are if you know what's good for you."

Jace let go of the hand in his mouth then reversed slowly, ready to pounce again if necessary. Louie did the same, and the pair of them sat at his feet, teeth bared.

"Get up," Sergeant said.

Staggering to his feet, hands dripping blood, their captive did as he'd been told.

"Identification," Sergeant said.

It was standard practice to ask for this when a stranger was on the grounds—if that stranger hadn't identified himself first. With no other shifter in human form to tell Sergeant this guy hadn't given up his name yet, protocol would be followed.

"Fuck you!" he spat at Sergeant.

Jace and Louie lunged forward, filling their mouths with those hands again.

"All right! All right! Jesus fucking Christ, let me go. I'll get it, I'll get it, goddamn you."

Jace and Louie sat once again.

The man produced a wallet. He tossed it at Sergeant's feet, and Jace wondered if a play had been made, a challenge put down. Did he really think, with all these wolves, he'd get anywhere *near* Sergeant?

Sergeant swiped up the wallet. He opened it then pulled out a driver's license. "Like I thought. Crossways Compound. Welcome to Highgate, Alpha Bennett. Can't say it's nice to meet you, but there you have it, a welcome of sorts all the same. You being here has just saved us one hell of a lot of trouble."

Jace wanted to dart forward and kill that son of a bitch for keeping his family imprisoned, for making his parents so unhappy they'd escaped, which had resulted in him being separated from them. From his brother and sister. He stopped himself owing to a look from Dillon, who stared at him with his coal-black eyes from across the circle. He knew what that look was conveying— *Remember the law. Don't take it into your own hands.*

Dillon shifted to human, his impressive body lithe as he walked over to a tree that had ivy snaking around its trunk. He yanked off a length of vine, stripping it of its leaves, then stalked to Bennett, who turned and looked at Dillon in disgust.

"Black bastard," Bennett said.

"Racist as well, are we?" Sergeant asked, his voice sharp.

"Only got whites on my compound, and that's the way it should be," Bennett said.

He curled his top lip, and as Dillon moved to secure his wrists with the vine, Bennett stepped forward. Dillon ignored him, kicking him in the back of one knee so Bennett went down. Dillon pushed his head, sending their guest sprawling forward. On his knees between Bennett's legs, Dillon did what he'd set out to do—he bound that fucker's wrists, and all without a word.

Jace wanted to cheer. His surrogate 'mother' had had such dignity in how he'd handled that bastard. Shit, Jace had been fortunate to have Dillon in his life.

"Haul him up," Sergeant said. Then he gave Bennett a hard stare. "And if you so much as think of shifting, we'll be on your ass like flies on shit, got it?"

Seemingly resigned, Bennett relaxed his shoulders and allowed himself to be led out of the woods and into the clearing. Three wolves took lead out front, three to each side, the rest following closely behind. Jace walked as near to Louie as he could, the enormity of what they'd been through skittering through him on wobbly legs.

Don't break down now. Wait until it's completely over.

The walk through the woods seemed to take forever, going at human pace. The sun was at the noon position, and Jace inwardly chuffed at the thought that they'd be having a very different kind of meeting now. He suspected Alpha Newart would be called to collect Bennett, and that after interrogation by Sergeant, Bennett would be taken away to the Knightly Institute.

Jace thought about what Bennett's capture meant. Freedom for the shifters at Crossways? Or were there others of like mind there as Bennett had implied, ready to take over where he had left off? Bennett would basically be imprisoned until his trial, and if found guilty—which he would be, Jace was sure—he'd return to a cell much like those jails the fulls had, where he'd serve whatever time was deemed necessary.

A whole lifetime if I had my way. If he's let out again, he'll just return to the kind of life he's led so far.

They emerged from the woods onto the lawn at the back of the compound, greeted by glorious sunshine. A row of wolves sat in front of the rear porch, pretty much every other adult pack member as far as Jace could see. Their solidarity touched him—how come he'd never really seen that before?—and once again he was ashamed of his previous behavior.

He'd changed now, though, and planned to make up for all the years he'd given people grief. There were many apologies to make—and hopefully Sergeant would let him speak to the pack as a whole when this was over, so he could explain himself only once. And also save himself the embarrassment of anyone not accepting his apology. Saying that, no one here at Highgate had ever been mean to him—not to his face anyway.

All of them have been so nice. Every single one.

It made his attitude all the more revolting.

I'll fix it. I will.

Pride swelled inside him as all the wolves stood then moved forward, enclosing Sergeant, Dillon and Bennett in a circle, as was their way.

"Meet *Mr* Bennett," Sergeant said, his lack of the word alpha highly significant. "He was an alpha, although in my opinion he's never deserved that status. He'll be staying with us until Alpha Newart arrives. Would someone be so kind as to sort out bedding in one of the basement rooms, please?"

A gray wolf loped off, disappearing into the pack house.

"Could a few of you prepare some refreshments? I'm sorry that your Saturday has been disturbed by such a son of a bitch, but it can't be helped. We'll need enough coffee and tea for the members who were back-up for the distress call, plus for Jace and Louie, myself and Dillon. And"—he sighed—"for Bennett. Thank you."

As three brown wolves made their way into the pack house, Jace caught a glint of white at the far left of the circle. So Kip was out here too. And Vann, sitting a head taller than the others, who nodded at Jace, and if Jace wasn't mistaken, Vann shook too. From anger?

Fear of Bennett? Kip blinked, his teal eyes sparkling with moisture, and Jace had the sad idea Kip was overcome with relief that Bennett had been caught.

What the fuck must it have been like to live under Bennett's rule?

Jace, thank Christ, had been lucky enough to never know, but had he not wandered off as a cub...

The circle of wolves broke apart at the topmost curve, creating a path for Sergeant and Dillon to guide Bennett through. They went into the main house, heading for the dining room Jace supposed, and the wolves followed them inside. Jace waited so he could be alone with Louie, who had stuck by his side the whole journey back. Jerking his head—*come on*—Jace led Louie round the side of the pack house, where he shifted and waited for Louie to join him in human form.

Jace pushed Louie against the house, flowerbeds be damned, and kissed him hard. He needed the contact, to show Louie that, shit, he was glad he'd had his back, that they were together, that he'd never had to step foot on Crossways, that he was here, with him, where he always wanted to be.

He pulled back, breathless. "Don't ever fucking leave me," Jace said, shaking Louie by the shoulder. "Ever. I can't live without you."

"I won't," Louie said. "I promise you, I won't."

Chapter Eight

After their emotional kiss, Louie was a bit narked at being back in wolf form, sitting in the outermost ring of their community circle around the table where Sergeant and Bennett sat. The room was crowded, the smell of fur prominent, overtaking that of coffee brewing and some kind of cookie being baked. The wolves hadn't shifted to drink, instead lapping from dog bowls placed on the floor before Bennett had been allowed into the dining room. The least amount of human faces Bennett saw to recognize later — if he were set free — the better. So far, all he'd seen as humans were Dillon and Sergeant.

Bennett had a plastic cup with juice in it — sensible, seeing as coffee was hot and a ceramic mug could be smashed and used as a weapon. Not that Bennett would get very far with that. There were too many wolves around, but it didn't hurt to be careful. He'd had the vine taken off his wrists too and kept his hands in his lap. His gun had been removed prior to him being seated, along with other weapons concealed in his clothing. Another gun inside his boot. A knife in a sheath strapped to his leg. This guy had meant business, well prepared to hurt them all if he'd had the chance. What sort of man was he to want to do that to his kind?

Shouldn't all wolves want to stand together, united, regardless of which pack they belong to?

Dillon stood behind Sergeant's chair, naked in case he needed to shift, Louie supposed. Sergeant was also naked, apparently unfazed by interrogating someone in the buff. Alpha Newart was en route, estimated time of arrival two p.m.

Another hour, then.

For the previous sixty minutes, Bennett hadn't said a word. Sergeant's questions had been relentless, yet their guest was resolute in remaining silent. Louie had never seen a more stubborn man—except maybe for Jace.

There was a shuffle to the right, and Vann shifted into human, standing tall behind a three-deep row of dark wolves. They reminded Louie of an ocean of fur, their calm surface milliseconds away from becoming angry, violent waves if Bennett stepped one foot out of line.

"I wondered when you'd show yourself," Bennett said, glaring across at Vann. "I knew you were here. Could smell you a mile off, you filthy little runt." He smiled, a creepy stretch of the lips that made him appear even more sinister. "Your mother's sick, by the way. Unfortunate case of food poisoning. Funny, that... You just can't tell with chicken, can you? I left her in the care of Wickland—as you know, a kind man just like myself." He laughed bitterly. "If she gets through her fever she'll be fine. If not..." He shrugged. "No fucking loss. The bitch deserves to die for bringing her three brats into the world."

Jace went to shoot forward, but the wolves in front moved closer to one another so that Jace would have to leap over them if he insisted on whatever plan was going through his mind. It was obvious to Louie — Jace wanted to rip Bennett apart.

"How are my sister and father, Alpha Bennett, sir?" Vann asked, miraculously keeping his voice steady and strong. "Are they sick too?"

"No." Bennett smiled again, showing yellow, tobacco-stained teeth this time. "Not yet, but they can be, if you want?"

"No, thank you, sir. I'd rather they remained well."

Louie was fucked if he'd call that man by the title of sir if he were Vann, but he reckoned old habits died hard. If Sergeant suddenly decided he should be called Alpha, it'd take a while for Louie to get it right.

"Besides, your father's too important to be ill, you know that. Can't have *him* being sick." Bennett smirked, those teeth of his glinting with spittle, yellow, haphazard tombstones in a foul black cemetery of a mouth.

"That thing you have him doing, it isn't right, sir," Vann said. "And it'll be stopped now that other people know about it."

"Thing?" Bennett asked. "I have no idea what you're talking about."

"Don't give me that crap." Vann straightened his shoulders. "I've already told Sergeant what you're up to. Those children… They're in pain. How can you sit by and let that happen?"

Children? What's Vann talking about?

Bennett snorted. "Because once they give in and shift, there'll be a new race, *that's* how I can let it happen!" He scraped his chair back as he stood. "And, you fucking bastard, look what you just made me say."

"You always were a braggart, sir," Vann said before shifting into his animal again.

Wolves growled, ensuring Bennett slumped back into his chair.

"A new race?" Sergeant asked. "Care to explain?"

"No, I fucking well don't care to explain." Bennett lowered his chin to his chest.

Kids in pain? Because they're staving off shifting? Why would they want to do that? Shifting's natural. How can they stop themselves from changing?

Louie couldn't imagine such a thing. Shifting was one of the first things babies did once born—after bawling their eyes out. How had these children not done that? What was stopping them? Strength of will? No, that couldn't be the case. Babies didn't have the capability to stop themselves shifting. And how old were these kids? Had they ever shifted?

"I know everything anyway," Sergeant said. "You've been a prick and mated wolves with lions, haven't you? Messed with the DNA so bad the cubs *can't* shift because their bodies are fighting with each side of their inner beast—wolf or lion? You're hurting them every time the desire to shift takes over. Literally torturing them. But I guess that's your thing, isn't it? Inflicting pain?"

Bennett didn't answer.

Oh, my God...

Sergeant shook his head. "Maybe Vann's father will find a way to help them—some kind of antidote that can be injected daily so they don't feel the need to shift. He'll be offered the best scientists to help him now, you know that, right? All your *work* undone, all your dreams unrealized while you rot in a goddamn cell. And may you rot in as much agony as those kids have been through." He slapped one hand onto the table. "Recuff the bastard and take him down to the basement. I've had enough."

Dillon applied a cable tie so tight Bennett's skin bulged either side of the plastic strip. So long as he didn't shift until he was in the basement, that was cool. If he shifted once down there, a Taser would be used to subdue him when Alpha Newart arrived to pick him up.

Louie wanted Bennett off the compound in the worst way.

Hauled to his feet by Dillon, Bennett was then marched out of the dining room, followed by Sergeant and several wolves. Once a couple of minutes had passed and the sound of the basement door creaking open reached the room, everyone seemed to shift into humans all at the same time. People looked round at one another, their eyes glazed, rolling shoulders and flicking hands to work out the kinks from sitting for so long. There was an air of sorrow hanging around them — the kids and their plight, Louie thought.

He turned to see Jace shaking his head as Vann moved toward him. What, he didn't want to speak to his brother? Or was he just trying to assimilate all the information? What must it be like to have a father who had been a participant — albeit against his will, Louie was sure — in a mixed-breed experiment? He dreaded to think. His own father had died years ago, his mother following soon after from a broken heart. He barely remembered what they looked like now unless he got out his old photos, but if he found out his father had done something like this, how would he feel?

I don't know.

"It wasn't his fault, Jace," Vann said. "Living at Crossways... You didn't shit without permission, you know?"

"I guess." Jace appeared dumbfounded. "Will he — our father — be able to help the cubs? Do they have any parents to care for them?"

Vann lowered his head to stare at the floor. "Once."

"Once?" Jace cocked his head.

"After they were born — all five of them to the same woman, who was forced to have sex with a lion shifter — she was killed."

"*What?*" Louie said, shocked to shit that something like this had been allowed to happen. "Killed?"

Vann nodded, reaching out his hand for Kip's as his lover stepped up to his side. "She was Kip's mother too. So not only was she too old to cope with childbirth again..."

"Oh my fucking God," Jace said, his face turning the wrong shade of green. "I'm so sorry." He touched Kip's arm. "So sorry that my father had something to do with this."

Kip looked up at Vann.

"You may speak," Vann said.

"It's okay." Kip's voice was surprisingly deep for such a small, slender man. "He is a good man, an honorable man. He had no choice. If you only knew what Bennett is like... And now there's Wickland to take his place. I'm afraid these experiments won't be stopped unless Wickland is caught and taken away. Wickland will continue — he's Bennett's twisted brother."

Horror filled Louie at the same time as the need to get to Crossways and do something about the terrible things that were going on there. Suddenly it wasn't just about freeing captives. Now there were children in agony, with no parents and —

"Who looks after the children?" Louie asked, dreading the answer.

"They're in cells," Kip said.

"Fucking hell," Jace muttered.

Louie paced now that quite a few pack members had vacated. Others hung around to listen to their conversation, and varying gasps ebbed and flowed around the room. The sounds of people sorting lunch in the kitchen filtered through, but Louie wasn't hungry.

"So you have five half-siblings who need taking in," Jace said to Kip. He looked at Louie. "We can do that between us, can't we? Care for them?"

He looked at Louie with such pain in his eyes that Louie couldn't refuse him. Was life about to repeat itself with Louie and Jace taking on a child as Sergeant and Dillon had done?

"If that's what you want," Louie said. "But I bet Alpha Newart will take them, get them the best care. Find them foster parents," Louie said. "But if we're needed, yeah, we can definitely do that."

Kip turned away to walk over to the window. Vann joined him, placing a hand on his back and rubbing circles.

"What a fucking mess," Louie said, grasping Jace's hand. "But it'll get sorted. Sergeant and Alpha Newart will make sure of it. And your father — if he's that clever, he'll know how to help the children. Maybe he already knows but hasn't been able to administer medication through fear of getting caught."

Jace nodded, although he didn't seem convinced. He left the dining room. Louie wasn't sure whether to give him space or go with him. In the end, he opted for going out onto the porch, where Jace was dressing.

"I need to go home," Jace said. "To my apartment. I need…something normal to focus on instead of all this crap. It's too much."

"Want company?" Louie asked.

"Of course I do. Not that you're normal or anything." Jace grinned then tugged his T-shirt over his head.

Jace's attempt at humor tickled Louie, and he chuckled while he pulled his clothes out of the bin.

"Glad to see you're still on track for revealing your real self. It's good to hear you cracking jokes, great to see you smiling even though there's shit going on." Louie pulled on his trousers, deciding to carry the rest of his stuff to Jace's apartment.

"I think, despite all that's going on, if we didn't have some light relief from time to time, we'd go mad. I mean, look how crazy I was before I told you my secret. Always so moody. You know how I got."

"Do I ever." Louie flicked his top at Jace's midsection. "But like I said before, it's gone. Done and dusted. Time to move on." He gave a bittersweet smile. "And although the future's not too bright in some respects, it is for us, isn't it?"

"Yeah. We're solid. It's like… This is going to sound mad, but it's like now we've admitted how we feel, we're already most of the way there. That the mating bond is just the last thing to do. Know what I mean?"

Louie did. "And once that's done, can you imagine what it must be like? Shit, I've seen the way Sergeant and Dillon look at each other. It's something else, the bond. I've tried to put myself in their place, to really try to understand what goes on, but I doubt we'll know until we're in it, a proper pairing, you know?"

"Yeah." Jace reached out and took Louie's hand. Linked their fingers. "You want to find out?"

"What, now?" Louie's tummy somersaulted.

"Why not? We've got a couple of hours before we might be needed—and I'll admit I want to see Alpha Newart, see if he's some magical-looking wolf king or if he's just a regular guy. It'll be a while before he's done here. We have time, don't we?"

Louie laughed. "At the rate we come, we'll be done inside two minutes."

Jace blushed. "That'll get better with time too, I guess."

"Come on," Louie said. "We'll give it a go."

They walked hand in hand over the lawn toward Jace's apartment. It was so natural, being with Jace, and it felt as though they'd always been together. None of that keeping their distance bullshit and hiding their feelings. Louie regretted not telling Jace sooner so they could have mated years ago, but making up for lost time would be worth the wait. Louie had convinced himself on several occasions that they'd never get together at all, so now that they were?

Wow.

Jace let them in. He closed the door behind him then tossed his keys onto a small table in the hallway. Already Louie belonged here—more so than in his own place.

Home?

"Will I move in here?" he asked. "Or will you come to mine? Or shall we wait for another apartment to become available so it's both of ours?"

"I don't mind." Jace stopped in the living room doorway to lean on the jamb. "Home is wherever you are."

"Then we'll live here." Louie felt good about making the decision. Once their mating was done and he'd hauled his stuff over here, maybe Vann and Kip could have his apartment. "And if we've mated here... Seems fitting to stay, d'you think? Memories and all that?"

Jace nodded. "You scared?"

"Yeah. You?"

"Fuck, yeah." Louie bit his bottom lip, conscious that they didn't know what the hell they were doing and would have to rely on instinct, letting it carry them through.

"You think it hurts as much as they say it does?" Jace blinked several times.

"What, a cock up the ass or the mating bite?"

"Both." Jace ran a hand over his chin.

"I expect so. Our asses will burn like a son of a bitch and as for the bite, hell, you've been nipped a time or two by Sergeant in wolf form—how's that feel?" *Please say it was okay...*

"Painful." Jace grimaced.

"Shit."

"Yeah, shit."

Louie forced brightness. "Hey, we can wait, you know. Until it just happens naturally." He smiled to let Jace know he was all right with that—all right with any decision Jace might make. "I mean, at some point one of us is going to get feisty during sex and bite. Then the other will do the same and it'll be over. Think about it, we haven't had proper sex yet. Maybe we should try one thing at a time?"

Jace smiled. "Right. Ass first, bite later?"

Louie nodded. "You got it."

Chapter Nine

The bed was still unmade from when they'd left it that morning. Usually Jace kept house pretty good, but things hadn't exactly been normal the past twenty-odd hours. And they were only going to be getting back in it. That thought had him almost trembling, and he felt such a dick about it. He was a man, for fuck's sake, not some teenager. But just because he was a man it didn't mean he couldn't be reduced to feeling much younger, did it? As a kid he'd always thought that becoming an adult meant he wouldn't get scared, wouldn't be insecure and would magically know everything. It hadn't worked out that way, and he wondered, was life always a succession of continually overcoming fears as new things were discovered? When he was forty, would he still worry, still feel out of his depth at times?

He thought of Sergeant and Dillon. How they always seemed so with it, so strong and confident. Did they ever worry when they were alone, locked away from the rest of the pack? Did they only appear as though they had their shit together?

That must be what being an adult is all about.

Showing the world a different face to the one you saw in the mirror at times—the one no one else saw. The one that stared back at you with its expression of complete and utter fragility.

He stared at the bed again, the sight of it bringing on a flood of indecision.

Fuck. Who'll go in whose ass? Will we take turns? I don't know what the fuck I'm doing and it'll freak me out if I let it.

Sure, he'd watched porn, he'd seen sex scenes on TV, but it had all been so well choreographed—the entry and whose backside was being used done so smoothly, that he hadn't thought about it in any great detail. In real life, was anything ever said? Did he have to ask, or would it come naturally? What if, when they got down to it, he wasn't ready to be penetrated? And what if Louie wasn't? Did it matter if they never made it to that stage this time? Or ever?

No, it doesn't. Not to me, anyway. We should just take it step by step, see how it goes.

He thought back to how he'd been earlier, when Louie had been in the shower. Jace had found, once his libido was up, he'd said whatever had come into his mind. Yeah, it had startled him that he'd said what he had, but going with the flow had worked then, so why not now?

Because this seems staged, like one of those pornos or a sex date, pressure to perform.

He turned and smiled at Louie, who stood in the doorway staring at the bed. Was he thinking the same as Jace? Did Louie need encouragement? Jace to come out with all that sexy stuff so he could do what was asked of him and he didn't have to think? Did all relationships have one leader and one who obeyed?

So many fucking questions.

He smiled. *Fucking* questions. Yeah, they were about fucking all right.

He chastised himself again for not listening to Sergeant when he'd wanted to give him the talk about the birds and the bees.

Me and my stubborn ass.

And would his ass be stubborn? Would it clam up when Louie tried to fit his cock in? Jace would drive himself mad if he kept on like this, so he got on the bed and decided to do something he never thought he would. Be dominant and call the shots. If it covered up his insecurities, all for the good. And if he made a hash of it, well, Louie would forgive him. They were both at the same level, no one-upmanship here. They'd stumble through this together, like they'd promised.

"Get those goddamned jeans off," Jace said as he got on the bed. He settled into a comfortable position then unzipped his jeans. He tugged his cock out. He didn't know how he was doing this, but now he'd started he'd have to continue. He gripped his hardening dick and gave it a few good pulls.

Louie did as he'd been told. His trousers dropped to the floor around his ankles, and he stepped out of them then kicked them away.

"And get that cock of yours a bit harder," Jace said. "That's right. You jerk off like I'm doing." The thrill of domination went through him—who knew it could feel like this? "Look at that. Such a beautiful cock."

Louie swallowed, clearly trying to come to terms with this turn of events. "How do you do that?"

"Do what?"

"Switch yourself on like that? Talk to me like that without being embarrassed?"

"I don't know, but it works, right?"

Louie nodded, letting out a groan as he watched Jace playing with his cock.

"Did you used to think of me like this?" Jace asked. "Did you imagine me jerking off? Wishing I was thinking of you, that I called your name out when I spunked?"

"Fuck... Yeah, I did."

"And then you came, hot and sticky all over your hand, your belly?"

"I did. And... Already this is too much, man. It's too exciting. I can't seem to hold off—like it's there, wanting to come out already."

"Same here. Did we make it over two minutes this time?" Jace smiled, easing off on how tightly he gripped himself.

Louie panted. "I think so."

"Then we've already gone to the next level. Come here. I want to touch you. I want to lick that drip of cum off the tip of your dick."

Louie approached the bed.

"To the side," Jace said. "So I can lean over and..." He swiped his tongue over Louie's cock.

Louie juddered. "Oh, fuck, I..."

"Turn around," Jace ordered. "So you can't see me. Cool off for a bit."

With his back to Jace, Louie hung his arms by his sides and took a deep breath, his shoulders lifting with it. "That's better. I daren't touch myself. Damn cock's got a mind of its own."

Jace squeezed the end of his dick, waiting for the need to come to fuck right off. He counted to ten, wondering if Louie was doing the same. The hunger inside him hadn't abated, but the fierce swell of his cock subsided a little.

Only a little, though.

"Come here," Jace said, hoping he hadn't called Louie to him too soon.

Louie joined him on the bed. They lay on their sides facing one another, treacherous cocks seeking contact so they rested together. Even that had Jace's heart rate skyrocketing, his pulse thudding in places it had never thudded before. And the sound of it, so loud inside his head.

"Here," Jace said, pulling out a tube from beneath his pillow. He handed the lube to Louie. "Slick up your cock. I want you in my ass."

"Oh, Christ…" Louie panted—he was struggling so bad.

Louie squirted lube down the length of his dick, sucking in a breath as he smoothed it over—probably cold, it was always so damn cold. Before he could change his mind or let Louie work out that he was nervous as hell, Jace got up on his hands and knees. He parted his legs so there was ample room for Louie to fit between them.

"Lube my asshole," he said. "Then put those lovely fingers of yours inside."

Did Louie just whimper? Jace wasn't sure, but if he did, he hoped it was from the torture of pleasure and it wasn't a sound of disgust.

"You want to do that, right?" Jace asked, just to be sure. "Put your fingers then your cock in me?"

"Yeah, yeah, I do, but what if I don't *make* it into your ass? Just the thought of my fingers… I'm so far gone already."

Jace knew how that felt. His cock was pulsing, and his balls were so tight they bordered on being painful. A good kind of pain, though, something he found he liked.

"So just finger me enough to get me loose, yeah?" Jace looked over his shoulder. "You good with that?"

Louie nodded, his finger glistening with lube, his cock shiny and dripping with the stuff. He shuffled over, fitting himself between Jace's legs, then Jace couldn't see him properly anymore without getting a crick in his neck. So he hung his head, staring through his legs at Louie's, which were pressed together, the bottom curve of his balls just about visible.

Louie sighed. Then the stickiness of lube on his finger made contact with Jace's hole. His pucker contracted by itself, his cock bobbing in time with the spasms. He reached down, squeezed his dick again— *No way am I going to last…*

"Slide a finger in," Jace said, out of breath as though he'd been running. "Just like you do to yourself."

"It's so different, seeing it— I can't see my own ass, can't see what it looks like with my finger there. But this? Shit, this is something else."

Jace wished he could see, but maybe later he'd get the chance to play with Louie's ass.

"Tell me what it's like," Jace said. "What you see."

"It looks so tight, like if I slide my finger in it's going to clamp it."

Jace imagined that. "So slide it in. Find out."

Louie didn't hesitate. He pushed his finger in slowly, releasing a hiss of breath through what sounded like clenched teeth. Jace sucked air in, holding it and closing his eyes tight. Jesus, why did it feel so different with someone else doing that? Louie found Jace's prostate straight away, and fuck, the back and forth glides over it almost had Jace coming. Everything was exciting—from being naked to being close and to being so revved up he couldn't stand it.

"Get that finger out and stick your cock in," Jace said, eager to experience thickness in his hole, something more than just a slender finger.

Louie pulled out, and the feeling of emptiness was not only in Jace's backside but in *him*, a hollow sense in his belly he'd never felt before. He didn't feel whole, didn't feel like himself anymore.

"Quickly," he ordered, knowing it was going to hurt because he hadn't been stretched enough. But he didn't give a fuck.

The pressure of hard softness at his pucker gave rise to a wave of exhilaration. It sped through Jace. Ripples of goosebumps erupted on his skin, sending him cold then hot. He snapped his eyes open, staring at the pillow, wondering if he'd need to dip his head in the next few seconds and bite the damn thing.

No, save the bite for Louie.

"Wait!" Jace said. He turned over, spreading his bent legs, holding his thighs close to his stomach, his knees at his chest. "If we both need to bite… Easier this way."

Was that the right thing to do? Would Louie be able to perform now they were facing one another? The look on Louie's face said he was maybe under pressure, that eye contact, of Louie being watched, would affect him.

Jace closed his eyes. "Go on. Please. Just do it."

Again that pressure at his hole—it was daunting. More pressure, stronger, his ass resisting. Then what felt like Louie's whole cock surged in.

"You're in?" Jace asked.

"Only the end, man."

Only the end? Oh, Christ…

"Push it in, all of it," Jace said, panting, hoping he wouldn't cry out and make himself look stupid. "Just do it all at once."

"I don't want to hurt you. Isn't it hurting already? It must be."

Yeah, it was hurting, but Jace knew if they didn't get this part done quickly, he might back out. "Do it already. Please."

Jace gritted his teeth and prepared himself. He bore down, knowing from when he'd fingered himself that it was the best way to allow entry. Louie obeyed, and the quick thrust seemed to go on forever. The stretch and burn, the pain — it was like no other. He felt full — too full, as though he needed to expel that cock, get it the hell out. Was this what it was like all the time? Was this what sex in the ass was about?

"You okay?" Louie asked.

Jace resisted opening his eyes. He didn't want to see the concern that was undoubtedly on Louie's face. If Jace told him it was hurting, they'd never continue.

Maybe this isn't for me. Maybe only one of us will like it up the ass. But when I finger myself, it's... I love that so...

"Yeah, I'm okay," Jace said. "You?"

"I'm struggling to hold off."

"So move — Come."

And Louie moved, the lube aiding the slide. Jace relaxed, let tension ooze out of him, and it made a huge difference. Although the stretch and burn were still there, it was lessened somehow, his rim getting used to it.

"Ah, fuck!" Louie said.

Louie sped up. His cock rubbing against Jace's prostate brought on the strongest need to come. He reached out blindly to take hold of Louie's arms and draw him down so their chests were flush. Louie's belly, which was clamped so close, massaged Jace's cock, switching his attention from his burning ass to the pleasure spreading through his dick. Louie moved even faster, shouted something Jace didn't understand, and his dick thickened, pushing Jace's rim to its limit. Louie kissed him, long and hard. Jace pressed his hands to Louie's back, wanting them to become one person. The need for that grew inside him, overwhelming in its intensity. All the love he'd felt for Louie throughout the years coalesced, forming a tight ball in his chest that made it difficult to breathe.

Jace snatched his mouth away and opened his eyes. "Look at me," he said.

Louie opened *his* eyes. They were damp.

"This is it, isn't it?" Louie asked, slowing his speed. "I've got something going on, like...like I want to scream out that I love you. It's hurting. Fucking *hurting* me, man." He paused, then, with his eyes half closed, he pounded into Jace. "Ah, shit!"

Louie dipped his head, latching his mouth onto the soft spot just above Jace's collarbone.

Yeah, this is it. We're mates — mates!

Louie bit.

The sensation of his teeth breaking through Jace's skin sent Jace to another place. His head spun, and he lost the ability to keep his legs bent up. He flung them out, keeping them wide, and let them rest on the bed. An *urge* came from nowhere, an inexplicable *need* to bite in return. He chose the same spot on Louie and sank his teeth in, all the while clutching at Louie like he never wanted to let him go. And he didn't — ever.

Then shit got real. Lust and love *whumped* into him, stronger than before, bolting around inside him, darting in all directions at once. Jace was full of it. The emotion of the moment promised to make him black out, so he fought to stay alert.

"We did it," Louie thought—thought or said? *"And Christ, I fucking love you."*

"I love you too. Can you hear me? I fucking love you too."

"I hear you. And you're mine, you got that? No one else's. Never have been, never will be. It's just us, me and you."

"Yes, yes. Me and you."

Wet heat filled Jace's arse at the same time that his feelings for Louie overwhelmed him. A lump bounded into his throat, and he couldn't seem to make himself stop biting. A faint whisper questioned whether he was hurting Louie, but Jace went by what he felt on his own collarbone and there was nothing but numbness.

Love, adoration, every goddamned word associated with caring packed inside Jace—so much so he thought he might burst with it. He came, finally breaking his mouth away to cry out, the sound more of a wolf's howl than a man. Louie unlatched his mouth too, snarling as he pressed his cheek to Jace's and shuddered through his orgasm.

This was heaven.

This was the start of his new life.

Chapter Ten

Louie couldn't get over how different he felt. More like a man than a floundering mess. It was as though he was finally in proper adulthood, something he'd thought would always be elusive if he didn't get with Jace. He'd taken a step—no, a leap—into a place he'd only dreamt of, and now he was there it was the best goddamn feeling.

I love him so much it hurts.

In the shower, they'd explored and kissed and touched and *felt*, and after eating, they were in the living room, Louie wondering if they'd ever speak out loud to each other in private again. The thought speech was addictive—would he ever get over how awesome it was?

"Can you still hear me?" Jace asked.

Louie smiled. He'd thought, in an idle moment during lunch, whether this new ability would wear off, or break, stop, sending them back to how they were. He'd questioned Jace repeatedly, or just said random crap to test it out. Jace had responded every time, yet it still hadn't eased Louie's worry over losing their novel bond.

"Yeah." Louie smiled wider. *"I was thinking – it's a good job no one else can hear what we're saying. I mean, there might be times you want to get all dominant on me in public. You know, say stuff like you want to suck my dick."*

Jace laughed. *"Can you see the pack's reaction to that?"*

Louie envisaged Sergeant's eyebrows shooting up and his mouth dropping open. Louie cracked up, so content and happy — so relaxed. Being mated was all he'd wished for and more. Bonding with a soul mate was unlike anything he'd envisaged. He'd thought about it in the past and now realized he hadn't quite gotten the real gist of it, the enormity of his feelings, the depth of them. Somehow, it was as though Jace was in him, flowing right along with his blood. Strains of Jace seemed to float into his mind, giving Louie pause, forcing him to consider other options, other answers than what he'd usually choose.

"Do you feel me in you?" Louie asked. *"Like, am I inside you?"*

Jace smirked. *"It still feels like you're in my ass, if that's what you mean."*

A flurry of disappointment hit Louie — snowflakes floating and dancing — and he turned his head to stare through the window. Maybe he just imagined Jace inside him. Maybe it worked differently for other people. He glanced at Jace again. The smirk fell from his face.

"Shit, Louie, I was only messing around. Yeah, I feel you." He gripped Louie's hand. *"And it's amazing. Just think, even when we're apart, we'll be together. Like you'll be with me, some of my conscience, helping me to make decisions. You got that too?"*

The way Jace had put it was spot on.

Louie nodded. *"It won't beat actually being together, but I love the idea of us never being alone."* A thought hit him then, sudden and cruel. *"And... And now I understand how mates know when... Well, when the other has died."*

Jace held his hand tighter. *"Don't. I can't even think about that kind of thing. Not when we've just got together."*

"I'm sorry." Mind talk wasn't right here, not for this kind of subject. "I shouldn't be thinking maudlin crap, but I love you so much I can't stand the idea of you not being there. It was bad before, when I thought we'd never get together let alone experience this, but now?" He leaped up to straddle Jace, tucking his arms behind his back to hold him close. Shit, that felt good. "Now"—he buried his face in Jace's neck—"it's unbearable. Don't leave me. Don't ever leave me."

Jace pushed Louie back a bit and stared into his eyes. "That's not up for negotiation, got it? Never—I will *never* leave you. I can't. You're me now, see? In my body, my head. I have no fucking clue how I lived before without you in there." He thumped his chest over his heart. "In here. Understand what I'm trying to say? We're not like fulls, where we love then fall out of it, where, when we get bored or start to think we've picked the wrong person we can just throw it all away and find someone else." Jace cupped Louie's cheeks. "This is it, this is our lot. We're *meant*, yeah? We had no choice, destiny dished out our bond, and she got it so right choosing to pair us."

Louie couldn't answer. Jace had said everything Louie would have said—if his throat hadn't all but closed with sentiment. He kissed Jace, pouring every ounce of love he felt into it, hoping it went inside Jace and stayed there too, a constant reminder when Jace got down that he was cared for, adored, and that Louie had his back no matter what.

"I felt all that," Jace said. "What you just thought. And I feel the same way. I'm here for you—always."

"I heard it evolves with time—you know, this sharing of feelings thing—but shit, it's happening so fast. How did we manage before? How did we think we were living?"

"I didn't manage and I didn't think I was living." Jace kissed the tip of Louie's nose. "I was an angry, bitter moron who didn't know he had it good. Who didn't think he'd have it better because I was such a jerk I didn't reckon on you wanting me. I knew we were meant to be mates, I just didn't know if we'd ever get it together."

"I'll always want you." Louie meant that—Christ, he meant it.

They kissed, softly, with such tenderness Louie told himself not to break down. Mating had been surreal, overtaking him, removing his will and replacing it with its own, a kind of shift but not. All his dreams had come true, but with them had also come fear—fear so strong it could control him if he let it. Jace was one of his arms, his legs, half of his heart. To have either go missing, to not have them there anymore—he couldn't face that, couldn't handle it.

"*Stop it*," Jace said, holding him closer and swirling his tongue around Louie's. "*Just kiss me. Be in the moment. Stay strong in every moment and don't let yourself think 'what if?'. They don't belong here. Not with us. We're strong, and we'll get stronger, don't forget that.*"

"*I didn't think I could love you more than I did, but I do, and every second it seems to be greater. And it's so much that I worry I won't cope with it. Like there's too much, you know?*"

"I know, Louie, I know."

Louie surprised himself by pulling away then getting off the sofa. He stripped, embarrassment long gone. That eager part of Jace was in *him* now — Louie could say and do anything he wanted without blushing, he was sure of it. Jace stared up at him, wonder, as well as a smile, clear on his face.

Naked and already hard, Louie walked to the bedroom then returned with lube.

"My turn," he said, a spiral of courage wheeling through him. "*Your* dick in *my* ass."

Jace swallowed, grin fully fledged, and shucked out of his jeans. His cock was thick and ready, and Louie had no qualms anymore about taking it up his backside. He wanted it — needed it — and planned to get it.

Down on his knees between Jace's legs, Louie slathered lube on that sexy-as-fuck dick. He jerked Jace off with two hands, palms sliding. He watched his movements, taking in the way Jace's cock strained, how the tip grew a deeper shade of red as Louie picked the pace up. Jace dropped his head back and closed his eyes, spreading his fingers on the sofa either side of him. The ends went white as he pressed them into the cushions. Normally Louie would be content with just being with Jace, content with any contact, sexual or not, but something inside him pushed for more. Like he wouldn't be complete unless he *had* more.

He squirted extra lube onto Jace's cock then smoothed it all over. After climbing on Jace, he stayed on his knees and reached back to position Jace's tip at his hole. The width there, the density of it, had Louie panting. He'd had the experience of pushing into Jace's ass and knew how that felt now, but it was his turn to feel what Jace had. The stretch. The burn. And he couldn't wait. He lowered a bit, staring at Jace so he could see his reaction. Earlier, when Louie had driven into Jace's ass, the clamp had been intense. Jace needed to feel that, to *know* that feeling. Lucky for Louie, he'd get to feel what Jace did as well as the sensations in his own body. Double the emotions.

Lowering further, Louie bit his bottom lip and went for it. Jace's cock popped inside him, breaching the barrier with its thickness. Louie's rim protested — man, did it burn — but he went down fast, needing that cock to fill him in one deep plunge. Louie cried out. Jace did too. Fully seated, Louie kept still. He clenched his teeth, coaching himself through the stretch searing his hole, through the discomfort of having something in his ass that seemed so big, so *there*.

"Tight," Jace said. *"So fucking tight I want to come. You feel me pulsing?"*

That was it for Louie. He rested his hands on Jace's shoulders and rode him, slowly at first then with more speed until the heat numbed. Being able to control the penetration made it easier, and leaning forward eased some of the extreme pressure. And had Jace's cock stroking his prostate.

"Oh, fuck. Oh, fuck, this is… Jace, I'm going to come."

Louie's cock throbbed and his balls drew up. Cum pulsed out of Jace's cock, warming Louie's ass. Louie looked down. Jace reached across to take hold of Louie's dick. He pumped it in a strong fist, head still back, eyes still closed, and Louie was undone. He came, hard, his rhythm on Jace going haywire. Jace yelled out, another wolf-like howl. Louie felt Jace's orgasm inside him, seemed to feel everything Jace did, as though Louie's cock was in Jace's ass and not the other way around. The sensation of being fucked and also fucking brought on such a forceful spurt of cum his cock swelled further. The passion of this fuck blew his mind, and he grunted, whined, gasped for air, unsure what to do with himself.

"Just go with it, Louie. Let it take you."

Louie gave in, allowing his and Jace's emotions to spiral through him. That wash of love came again, so violent, so powerful he went weak with it. He couldn't ride Jace anymore, had to stop, to hold Jace close to his chest and just let the cum flow. It went on forever, or seemed to, and he shuddered with ecstasy, in goddamn seventh heaven. It took a second for him to realize Jace wasn't jerking him off anymore.

"Ah, Christ. Jesus, I... Jace, I can't think straight."

"Just hold me."

Jace wrapped his arms around Louie's back, and they held on to one another. Louie kept on coming, wishing it would stop yet hoping it would keep going.

"This is different. Is this it?" Jace thought. *"The true mating?"*

A memory briefly flounced into Louie's head, of when he'd overheard a conversation years ago how with true mating, the real deal, mates seemed to come and come with no end in sight.

"Yeah... Yeah, this is it, Jace."

So this was how it felt, to go on for longer than the usual thirty-second orgasm. Claiming and being claimed stormed through him, a kind of rage that swamped his whole body, possessing, altering his mind. New awareness surged into him from some outer reaches he'd never known existed, like a section of his brain had been empty all his life, waiting for this day so it could be filled with extra senses—filled with so much more than fulls would ever know. They were missing out on so much.

"I always thought there was no justice in my world." Jace gripped him tighter. *"But there is. It's you.* You're *my justice."*

Louie cried then. Fuck being a 'man' and holding it all in, acting like he was tough and things didn't get to him. They did, they were, and if he couldn't show that with Jace then what was the point? Silent as the tears streaked down his face, Louie convulsed, his cum spent but the bliss continuing. Jace pressed his cheek to Louie's chest, and Louie felt Jace's empathy, tears of his own wetting Louie's skin.

"You were what I needed all along, Louie. To show me I could smile, that happiness was there to be had. I lived in darkness, in torment, in pain. And now it's all gone. It's all fucking gone. I'm free."

Louie didn't need to reply. Instead, he let his response flow from him into Jace, knowing it flooded him, warmed him, confirmed that there *was* such a thing as destiny. For too long they hadn't fully believed, and to know that they'd been wrong to think they wouldn't be with each other was almost too much to comprehend.

"What if we hadn't gone to the pool, Louie? What if I hadn't told you my secret? We'd still be stuck back there, in that hateful place instead of here, where everything is so right. I've found myself in you. Can you feel it? Tell me you can feel it."

"I feel it. I feel you. I can't..." Louie's chest hitched and he struggled to breathe. *"I can't find the right words."*

"I hear them. I know them. I've got you – don't you worry, I've got you."

At last the wrath of orgasm abated, flowing away in soft pulses that left Louie wrung out. Tired. He relaxed his hold on Jace then climbed off him. On unsteady legs, he held out a hand. Jace took it, stood, then together they stumbled into the bedroom.

Beneath the covers, with Jace snuggled against his side, Louie held him, both arms wrapped around him, fingers interlaced. He didn't want to let him go, to have these feelings go. If it were possible, he'd stay like this forever, in this moment. The real world and everything in it could go to hell in a handbasket. All he cared about was them being together, their love and passion, the discovering of one another's bodies and thoughts and dreams. Every goddamn thing that they were and could be in the future.

He closed his eyes, his whole being content, his mind full of nothing but Jace, Jace, Jace. He felt Jace's exhaustion and knew they'd sleep and miss Alpha Newart's visit, but he didn't give a shit. What had seemed important before wasn't now. Not the trouble at Crossways, nothing. And he didn't even feel bad about thinking that. It wasn't that he didn't care about the cross-bred kids and those other pack members, he did, it was just that they had no place in his heart and mind right then. There was no room for them.

And who knew what he and Jace would be like when they woke? New people? Super aware? Their original selves but enhanced? Whatever they were, it didn't matter so long as they were together. For now, absolutely *nothing* mattered but them. He tried to form cohesive thoughts, to stay awake so they could meet Alpha Newart, but the ability was rapidly slipping away. Each time he latched onto something it floated off, dandelion fluff blown from the stem.

He knew one thing for sure, though.

Love wasn't a strong enough word to explain how he felt about Jace.

It just wasn't big enough. Four little letters. Even if a word could be made from the whole twenty-six in the alphabet, it wouldn't be adequate.

Chapter Eleven

The sound of stout knocking woke Jace. He leaped out of bed then headed for the front door, not caring that he was naked. For someone to be knocking like that, it had to be serious and clothes were by the by. The sound had an urgency to it, propelling him to act without thought. Did their mating have something to do with that? Had it made him different in some way other than the changes he'd already acknowledged? Was Louie's awesome sense of knowing when something wasn't right inside Jace too? Along with everything else about him?

Jace certainly felt different. Stronger. More aware. A better person.

Whole. Alive. Fresh and new.

He flung the door open to see Sergeant on his doorstep, looking him in the eye.

"You might want to get dressed," Sergeant said. "And clean the blood off you. The bite mark will be healed already underneath that crust, but the blood being there? Not a good look if you're thinking of wearing an open-neck shirt." He smiled. "Listen, joking aside, and I'm sorry to interrupt, but Alpha Newart will be leaving in a while and we're having a quick meeting before he goes. I want you two in on it."

Jace thought of how he'd wanted to apologize to the pack for how he'd behaved all his life. "Can I...?" He moved from foot to foot, embarrassed. "I need to apologize to everyone, so can I do it after, seeing as they'll all be in one place at the same time?"

"Apologize for what?" Sergeant frowned. "And shit, at least let me in, will you, if you're going to stand there starkers. Anyone could walk along the landing here. Unless you don't mind people seeing your pecker and knowing what you've been up to recently."

Jace stepped back to allow Sergeant entry. "I need to apologize for me being a prick all these years."

"Already done it for you, son. Folks came out to greet Alpha Newart, and while they were all gathered, I slipped it in that you were sorry. You'll get no backlash from them. They'll have me to deal with if you do. Besides, you should know the pack by now. They're a decent, loving bunch. No one will hold a grudge against you. I've let them know from time to time over the years that you just needed to find yourself and then you'd change. And I was right. You did change. You have—I can sense it right now. Comes off you in waves. Even your face looks different without that frown, although it's left faint lines where it's so used to being scrunched up." He closed the door to, chuckling.

"You shouldn't have to keep smoothing the way for me," Jace said. "But thank you."

"No problem. And smoothing the way is my job as your father. Or it was until you got with Louie. Now I reckon I'll have to step back, let you get on with things by yourself." He paused to sigh. "That's going to be tough. Look, it was never an imposition, taking you on, despite what you might think. I want you to know that. You completed mine and Dillon's lives, okay? We had a kid, something we didn't think we'd have. All right, a downright moody little kid, but a kid just the same. We love you, always will, end of story. And if you want to go and meet your real parents, don't hold back on our account. We knew this day would come, we prepared for it, but you'll always be our kid in our eyes." He dumped one hand on Jace's shoulder. "Now, before I start getting too emotional, clean up, get dressed. We'll all be in the dining room."

Sergeant left, and Jace stared through the open doorway, watching him take the stairs. Yet again he was reminded of how much Sergeant had done for him—Dillon too—and a slew of guilt attacked him. It roiled in his gut, making him feel a bit sick.

"What did I tell you?" Louie asked behind him.

Jace closed the door then turned. "I know." He sighed. "What's done is done. New start."

"Right. So do as your father said and clean that blood off."

Jace looked at Louie's collarbone. "I could say the same to you."

"You could, but we don't have time to throw orders back and forth. Come on."

After they'd showered and dressed, they left the apartment, Jace anxious at meeting Alpha Newart. That man ruled all of them from afar, and as there had never been cause for him to visit Highgate, Jace had only heard snippets of what he was about. He was apparently fair but strict with it, and if there were reasons a shifter had to be admonished by him, that shifter had been pretty damn bad. Jace had always imagined him as a big man because of that, as tall as Vann or Sergeant and just as imposing, yet the stranger he scented on the breeze as they walked across the lawn didn't give that impression.

In the dining room, wolves in human form filled every chair and some stood around the edges, others leaning against the walls. At the center table, Sergeant sat beside Dillon, three men opposite them. Two were blond and the other white-haired.

I forgot he'd be old.

Old wasn't the word. Wizened and ancient seemed more fitting. Alpha Newart, small in stature, either diminished by age or undersized in general like Kip, had his hands clasped on the table top. His skin, horse chestnut in color, wrinkled and tough-looking—as though he'd spent far too much of his life being a sun god or a tan-bed lover—enhanced the whiteness of his hair.

Sergeant turned to stare at Jace and Louie over his shoulder. "Ah, now that the last two of you are here…" He winked and stood then moved to stand at the far end of the room facing everyone.

Chairs scraped as pack members moved their chairs to face him.

"I've been in discussions with Alpha Newart and we've made some decisions," Sergeant said. "Alpha Newart will take Bennett back to Knightly Institute with the aid of Marcus and Robert here." He indicated the two blonds who sat with Alpha Newart. "Our plan of going to Crossways to free the pack there has been given our leader's blessing. Wickland—Bennett's brother and apparently just as nasty—will need subduing. Once he's caught, Alpha Newart will come to collect. Wickland will also be taken to Knightly. Any questions so far?"

No one said anything.

"Vann and Kip," Sergeant went on, "have requested that they be on the team going to Crossways. I had my reservations about that, but as Alpha Newart pointed out, our two new family members know the layout and will be a great help. Them knowing the pack there will also be to our advantage."

Jace's stomach clenched. He wasn't sure how he felt about Vann returning to Crossways. All right, they didn't have any kind of bond, but what if Jace never got the chance to get to know him, to even form a bond? Something might go wrong while the team were on their assignment and—

Don't think about it. It is what it is. Things have been decided and I can't stop them.

"I'll stay behind to take care of everyone here, as I've always done," Sergeant said. "I need to be around in case Wickland realizes what we're up to and sends some of his people here. Dillon will be leading the Crossways mission."

Dillon had been the less dominant of his parents, the one who had stayed somewhat in the background and let Sergeant mainly bring Jace up. But the thought of Dillon being harmed gave Jace pause to inspect his feelings, something he rarely did with regards to the men who had raised him. He didn't want Dillon to go. The big, dark man had always been a presence in his life, and to not see him out on a run or by Sergeant's side...

I'm going to miss him.

Jace swallowed down a protest. He was twenty-five, not five. He couldn't stamp his feet and blurt out that he didn't want one of his parents to leave him. And, more to the point, Jace had done what he'd always done. Thought about himself. How *he* felt shouldn't be his priority. What would Sergeant go through with Dillon gone? They'd never been parted before as far as Jace knew. He thought back to his conversation with Louie about a mate knowing when the other had died. What if Dillon—?

No. He'll come back safe. And Dillon and Sergeant can talk in thoughts, will know how the other is feeling. Sergeant can guide Dillon through it.

Jace felt better for that and returned his attention to the meeting. He'd missed hearing a lot of information while he'd yet again been wrapped up in himself.

"So," Sergeant said. "Any questions now?"

Many mumbled no, others shook their heads. As far as Jace could see, everyone looked at Dillon with sadness. It seemed no one wanted him to go. Dillon stood and gazed around at each person in turn, as though he wanted to imprint them all in his mind. He left Jace until last. His dark eyes seemed to be reflecting a need Dillon felt inside. For Jace to finally accept him.

"I love you and I'm sorry," Jace mouthed, the shame of his past behavior singeing his cheeks.

Dillon nodded then abruptly turned his glistening eyes away to address the crowd in general. "We leave immediately after this meeting." His voice sounded rusty, laden with emotion. Thick, as though he hadn't spoken in an age. "Xavier will take over my post here while I'm away. Anyone has any security issues, go to him. Thank you."

He strode from the room quickly, leaving not only silence behind him but the sense that the pack was broken, fractured somehow. Like they wouldn't be their usual solid unit without Dillon there. Had Dillon felt he was saying a final goodbye, that he'd never be coming back? A childish need rose in Jace—to go out there after him and fling himself into his arms.

He followed his instincts.

Dillon was on the porch, bent over, resting his forehead on arms that he'd balanced on the rail. He stood upright then turned as Jace approached. Jace went up to him, grabbed him in a bear hug, reduced to being a cub who needed reassurance.

"I'll be home soon, you know," Dillon said, patting Jace's back. "I can't *not* come back when my kid and mate are here."

"Fuck. I'm so sorry."

"No need to be. We understand, always did."

"I don't deserve you."

Dillon eased away to look at Jace. "Yes, you do. Like you deserve Sergeant and Louie, and now Vann and the rest of your biological family. Things will be all right from here on out, you'll see."

Jace believed him. He had to. The alternative wasn't something he would contemplate. He stared at Dillon's face, seeing wrinkles and the slight greying of hair at his temples—something he'd refused to really look at before.

And he knew—however unconventional it might seem to others—that *this* was his mother. One half of a set of parents who had given up so much for him—and who were continuing to do so when Dillon went to Crossways to set Jace's real family free.

"I'll never forget this," Jace said. "And I'll pay you back someday."

"You do that by being happy." Dillon let him go. "Because that's all we've ever wanted."

Jace gave him a wobbly smile. "I'm happy, see?"

"Then so am I. Go now. I don't do long, drawn-out goodbyes, not anymore."

Jace walked away, wondering what he'd meant by that and realizing that he didn't know much about Dillon's life prior to his time at Highgate at all.

When Dillon returned, Jace would remedy that.

And he will return, he's got to.

Jace wandered down the side of the house. He pressed his back to the wall and took a moment to steady himself. He just needed a few seconds to process his emotions. He closed his eyes. Sucked in a huge breath. So much had happened, so many feelings had swamped him recently that he suddenly felt tired. Bone weary and in need of a deep, sound sleep.

"Hey, you okay?" Louie asked.

Jace pushed off the wall, startled into opening his eyes, then remembered the mating bond. *"Yeah, I will be. I just needed a minute to…"*

"I know. I can feel it. Things will get sorted at Crossways and Dillon will come home. Then everything will be back to normal. Want company or would you rather be alone?"

"I'm not alone. You're with me. But yeah, I need you here now, beside me."

Louie poked his head around the corner of the house.

Jace laughed. "You knew damn well I'd say yes, didn't you?"

"Of course I did." Louie walked toward him, arms out.

Jace met him halfway, pressing his body to Louie's, a sense of being whole again encompassing him. It felt so good—more than good. "What Sergeant and Dillon are doing, being parted… I couldn't do it, could you?"

"No, but when you're an alpha, you take on certain responsibilities. Sergeant has to look after the pack, and sending Dillon is the only way to get this shit sorted. It's a sacrifice they knew he'd have to make at some point, I'm sure."

"If it wasn't for Bennett being such a prick, none of this would be happening."

Louie stroked Jace's head, the movements soothing, sending Jace toward drifting off to that place where only they existed. It tempted him so much he pulled away then steered them across the grass toward his apartment. No, *their* apartment.

"Hey, do you realize what you said back there?" Louie asked. "What you did?"

Jace frowned. "No, what?"

"You didn't take the blame. You didn't have yourself as the focus. You said '*If it wasn't for Bennett*'. Normally it would have been '*If it wasn't for me*'. Jeez, things *have* changed."

For a moment Jace nearly retaliated in the old way, with a mean stare full of hate directed at Louie before walking off to be by himself, but he caught it just in time. Yeah, things had changed all right, and they'd keep changing if he had anything to do with it.

"It's you," Jace said. "You've helped me to change."

And it'll be a constant journey until one day I reach the end of the road and find I've gone a whole day without thinking shitty things or acting like a bastard.

That day couldn't come soon enough, but he wasn't stupid, he knew that completely switching himself around after twenty-five years of being a different person would take time and patience.

"I've got that," Louie said. "Time and patience. And you're not a bastard, you never were. You were just mixed up. But I'll unmix you—or mix you up in another way entirely, if you know what I mean."

The glint in Louie's eyes said all that had to be said. No sensing what Louie felt, no hearing Louie's thoughts was needed here. Just that twinkle that screamed, 'Take me to bed and fuck my goddamn arse.'

"You heard my thoughts right," Louie said.

"And you're getting better at this sexual gig. You know, saying the kind of shit I've been coming out with."

"Oh, it's going to get better, believe me." Louie grinned. "I've got the balls to ask for whatever I want now that a part of you is inside me."

"Really, huh?" Jace raised his eyebrows.

"Yeah, really."

"Go on then. Tell me what you want," Jace challenged, thinking Louie would maybe back the hell out.

Louie stopped walking and waited for Jace to do the same. "What do I want, hmm? You sure you want to know?"

"Yeah. Put your money where your mouth is."

He's stalling. He won't be able to do it.

Louie smiled. "Oh, I will."

He stared directly at Jace, bold and meaning business. He tugged Jace closer. "I want you"—he licked Jace's lips—"to get down on your knees"—he slapped his hands onto Jace's ass—"and suck my cock so it touches the back of your throat"—he pushed his erection against Jace's groin—"and I want to come, filling your mouth and—"

"No more." Jace stepped back a bit and put a finger to Louie's lips. He glanced down at the bulge in Louie's jeans then stared at his own. "Don't say another smutty word." He glanced up at Louie's face. The look he got back melted his knees. "Fuck. You win." He jerked his thumb over his shoulder. "Just get your goddamn filthy little ass home."

VANN'S
VICTORY

Chapter One

Vann's stomach churned. The plane was coming in to land. He closed his eyes, shaking all over. What if they crashed? What if he never got to save the shifters at Crossways? More importantly, what if something went wrong, if there was an accident, and he never saw his mate, Kip, again? Should he be ashamed that this was his main fear? Losing Kip had always been one of his nightmares. Except he'd never thought it would be because of an accident. Or not an accident in the real sense of the word. No, an 'accident' designed by Bennett, that would be more like it.

He concentrated on that instead of the gut-knotting experience of landing. Bennett, the former alpha at Crossways, had forever been a looming, frightening presence in Vann's life and mind. One wrong step and Bennett would tell the rest of the pack to rip him apart until he was dead. Being caught with Kip in an uncompromising position would have been more than good reason for Bennett to order an execution. Hiding had been the name of their game.

He glanced across at Kip, who was staring out of the window. Vann should have known Kip would act like this, a kid in a candy store, soaking everything up and loving it. Kip had a brilliant zest for life, for living it the best way he could in any given circumstance. He looked on the bright side most of the time, something Vann had yet to learn.

Damned if I'll look out of that window.

Just the thought of seeing the land below, a patchwork quilt humanity had sewn together, had him feeling even worse. It would bring home how high they were, how far they'd fall if the plane ran into difficulty. Turbulence. A sudden storm. The idea of crashing freaked him the hell out.

Please, just let us touch the tarmac safely.

As it turned out, everything went smoothly and he needn't have worried. Funny how he got himself all coiled up over things then they turned out okay in the end. He supposed, what with his upbringing, he always expected the worst. It wasn't surprising. Bennett had ruled with an iron fist, and no one—no one—had disobeyed him. Vann wondered if he'd be able to change once this mission was over. If he'd learn to accept that life wasn't always doom and gloom—that there *was* goodness out there, ready for him to experience it. If only he had the courage. And life could be good, he'd seen that at Highgate. Bennett had a lot to answer for. How many of the Crossways pack felt just the same as Vann did? How many of them were frightened beneath their brash exteriors? He'd bet there were quite a few.

It's all over now. He's been caught. But Wickland hasn't. We still have him to deal with.

He straightened his shoulders as the plane touched down, and let out a long breath of relief.

And we will deal with him. I have to keep positive. Everything will be all right now we have the Highgate shifters on our side.

It seemed the time to get off the plane passed in a flash, and Vann's breath caught as he strode along the tunnel that led to the airport. He felt enclosed, claustrophobic, and coached himself to keep a level head. He had to admit that his first time on an aircraft hadn't been as awful as he'd expected, although he'd been scared shitless of getting on something so big. Yeah, he'd seen them flying over Crossways, but during his shielded childhood, he hadn't ever thought he'd end up getting inside one. He had no idea how they worked. His education was limited to English and math as he'd grown up, and that had been taught to him by his mother.

There's so much to experience. So much I don't know anything about, but hell, I can experience it now. Me and Kip together, taking on our new world.

The thought of it had Vann smiling.

Kip walked by his side, head bowed, as was his custom. God, Vann loved that little man. Kip was a slender, white-haired, tiny sub who preferred their sexual lifestyle to extend from the bedroom into their day-to-day lives. That had been a learning curve for Vann but he'd gotten used to it over time. The Highgate shifters probably thought their relationship odd, but he was past caring what they thought now. Highgate's alpha, Sergeant, had told his pack what Vann and Kip were about, and if they didn't like it? Well, that was their problem. The days of Vann wanting to be accepted were long gone. He loved Kip and vice versa, so what did the opinions of other people matter?

It felt good to finally be able to have their relationship out in the open.

For a blissful moment there, Vann's thoughts had been diverted from those that had filled his mind on the flight—their reason for being back this side of Texas. He'd known they'd return, of course he had—leaving his parents, sister Terena, and around ninety other pack members at the mercy of the new Crossways Compound's alpha wasn't an option. Wickland would have undoubtedly heard that their former alpha, his brother Bennett, had been taken to Knightly Institute by their overall ruler, Alpha Newart. Wickland would also have taken full command, being just as nasty as his brother, possibly even worse.

Vann shuddered.

Kip tugged at his sleeve. Vann peered down at him.

"You may speak." Vann was thankful for yet another diversion. "Although if it's private, don't forget to use thoughts instead."

"It's not private," Kip said, but he glanced around just the same to make sure their Highgate companions weren't listening. He moved closer, titling his head toward Vann. "Are you all right, Sir?"

"Not really, sub." Vann shrugged, reaching out to connect with Kip's mind. *I don't really want this discussion overheard. I know the Highgate men are a good bunch, but old habits... We're so used to having our conversations listened to at Crossways.*

He shuddered again. When the fuck would he feel normal, whatever that was? Would the day ever come where he wasn't constantly worrying over what he said and did?

During their brief stay at Highgate, the alpha there, Sergeant, had been so far removed from Bennett that he was like a sunny day compared to a storm. Sergeant was easy-going, just wanting the very best for his pack. Bennett was the opposite. Mean and wanting only complete compliance—and total control to the point pack members were never allowed to step off the compound.

Prison. That's where I've been all my life. Fucking prison.

Vann blew air out, ballooning his cheeks. *"We knew this would happen, us returning here. Or at least we hoped it would happen. We've got the Highgate pack on our side now, thank fuck. Coming back here alone, just you and me, and trying to free everyone... I reckon we were fools to even think it could work."*

"But we were desperate, Sir," Kip whispered as they entered the airport and made their way through to the main lounge.

Vann tensed, glancing around the terminal in all directions, keen to spot anyone from Crossways who had come to fetch them. The place wasn't packed out, thankfully, only a few people dotted here and there on seats while they waited for their flights to be called. He recognized no one, but that didn't mean anything. Who knew whether extra recruits had been brought into Crossways, people Vann had never met? With Dillon, Sergeant's mate, walking ahead of them, he doubted any Crossways member would have the balls to step forward to claim Vann and Kip, but still...

I wouldn't approach Dillon. Fuck, he's a shadow mountain, his eyes so bright in that dark face of his. When I first saw him...man, he shit the life out of me.

Maybe that was why Sergeant had put Dillon in charge of this mission. Anyone willing to tackle him would *have* to be brave.

Dillon headed for the main doors that led outside. They had no heavy luggage—they didn't plan on being here for long—each of them carrying a holdall with a change of clothes inside. Vann's and Kip's held items Sergeant had found for them, seeing as they'd turned up at Highgate as wolves.

Vann's feet and legs ached, as if to remind him that they'd trekked across Texas to find his brother, Jace— endless days on foot and feasting on wildlife so they didn't starve, drinking from streams. They'd slept fitfully during the night, hiding in woods or on roadsides that, if they'd been lucky to find them, had trenches that had given them some kind of security.

It seemed a lifetime ago that they'd made that journey.

Dillon held up one hand. Everyone from Highgate stopped behind him. There were ten of them in all. Vann hadn't spoken to the others on the flight, but he'd listened as they'd gone over and over their plan of attack. It was a sound one, something Vann could imagine them pulling off well.

Providing Wickland was subdued first.

Dillon turned to face them, his eyebrows drawn together. "As you know," he said quietly, leaning forward, "after I've been out to one of the cabs and give you the signal, we leave here and walk the short distance to our left where there's a hotel. I'll sign us all in then we'll each go to our respective rooms. We rest up until dinner, which I believe is served at eight. We'll talk more in the dining room. If we encounter resistance along the way, or even in the hotel, you know what to do."

Vann thought about the sports bag that should be in one of the cabs outside those glass doors. Alpha Newart had arranged for it to be delivered. It contained small bags that held Tasers, something Vann had never used and never thought he would.

He'd only ever seen them on TV. But in order to release the Crossways pack, he'd *have* to use one, no getting out of it.

"I'll hopefully give the signal in a moment or two," Dillon said.

He pushed one of the glass doors open then went outside. A driver four cars up in the snake of a cab queue waved a beefy hand, his bare, hairy arm thick and tanned. Dillon walked forward and Vann held his breath, praying no one from Crossways had gotten wind of the Taser handover and fucked everything up. The driver jerked his thumb into the back of his car. Was this where it all went wrong? Was someone in the back, waiting to drag Dillon inside?

Torn between watching Dillon and scoping the airport lounge again, Vann released his breath. Dillon opened the cab door, leaned in then pulled his head out, bag in hand.

A collective sigh of relief sounded, and Vann realized everyone here from Highgate had thought the same as him. Jesus, he was surprised they weren't all a bag of nerves. And if they were like this now, what the fuck would they be like at Crossways?

Dillon closed the cab door then looked around. He lifted a hand to scratch his head — the signal — and one of the Highgate guys came forward from behind Vann to push the airport door open. He was a stocky, burly, black-haired guy, wider than Vann and packed with muscle. He stepped out onto the pavement, scanned the area then ushered everyone outside.

They followed Dillon down the path to a bench. There, Dillon hoisted the bag on top. He opened it, and each member of the mission crew dipped a hand inside to take out a smaller bag. Vann gripped his tightly, thinking that if they were ambushed now,

none of them would have time to draw back the zips
and pull out the Tasers. He glanced around nervously,
hoping airport security weren't watching. He spotted
a camera over the road on a post in front of the car
park. It was moving from its position of pointing at
the airport doors, toward them.

"Camera," Vann said. "Quickly."

Dillon hung the sports bag on his shoulder and they
walked on. Vann studied their group, his stomach in
knots. The Taser bags looked like ones that came with
hand-held cameras. Did the mission men appear as
tourists? A bunch of guys maybe here for a bachelor
party? He could only hope that was the case.

The hotel loomed before them, tall and majestic with
its glass and chrome façade reflecting the sun, which
didn't seem to want to go to bed any time soon. Vann
wanted *his* bed or at least a chair to sit on—his feet
were still killing him—and was glad their mission
wouldn't begin until two a.m. They needed the cover
of darkness to aid them.

When Dillon reached the hotel doors, Vann let out
another breath he hadn't realized he'd been holding.
With Kip in his peripheral, Vann waited their turn to
enter. The sun's heat was intense on the back of his
neck, and sweat soaked his T-shirt. He wanted a cool
shower. The thought of it almost had him whimpering
with longing.

Kip tugged at Vann's sleeve again. Vann nodded.

"Shall I wash you, Sir? When you get in the shower?"

"If that's what you want. Thank you."

"You're welcome, Sir."

Dillon entered the hotel. Their group followed, and
the conditioned air was cold compared to outside. The
sweat dried on Vann's skin immediately, leaving it
tight and uncomfortable. Everyone but Dillon sat on

the seating in the foyer, as had been discussed on the plane. Vann looked around, seeking out spots where people could be hiding. The Highgate men did the same. Kip, however, bent his head and stared at the floor.

God, he loved Kip. His sub had such belief in him, even to the point of always entrusting his safety to Vann. This was no ordinary thing they were doing, but then again, neither was living at Crossways, and Kip had been the same there. Bennett's men had lurked in hallways, ready to pounce out at Vann and Kip if they'd managed to grab some time alone.

Vann switched his attention back to the present. He shouldn't keep allowing his mind to wander like that. And he needed to shield those types of thoughts more often. Kip didn't need to hear that sort of crap. With Kip trusting him the way he did, Vann was doing him a disservice. Vann had promised to take care of him, to love him and make sure he came to no harm. Thinking about their life at Crossways while he was supposed to be checking out the hotel foyer wasn't something he ought to be doing.

Focus. Our lives depend on it.

Dillon came to stand beside their chairs. He emitted a vibe, as though energy and purpose filtered out of him and into the air, suffusing everyone in his presence. The man seemed to be comfortable with himself and who he was. Vann hoped to be the same one day. Self-assured, confident. Dillon jerked his chin up then stalked away. Everyone followed him. The elevator arrived and they all stepped on board. Again, no one spoke. Vann opened his Taser bag, as did everyone else. Tense as the elevator stopped on their floor, Vann offered up a silent prayer.

Please, God, let there be no one in this hallway.

The elevator dinged. The doors slid open. Dillon eased out like a policeman or a seasoned army officer, Taser held out in front of him. Just what had he been employed as before he'd gone to Highgate? Whatever it was, Vann was grateful for the obvious training he'd had. Dillon was Head of Security at Highgate and Vann could see why. The man knew what he was doing as he went out into the hallway and scouted the area, pointing the Taser every which way before lowering it and giving the all clear.

Everyone vacated. Dillon nodded, giving the signal that he was about to check all their rooms. The laborious yet important wait while he did that further played on Vann's nerves, but it was necessary. Being unable to help also pissed Vann off a bit. He was used to doing what Dillon was, checking everything was safe. But from what Vann could see, Dillon clearly wasn't the type to leave anything to chance. Just like Vann.

Rooms cleared, Dillon handed out the key cards without saying a word then disappeared into number one hundred and four. Vann led Kip to one hundred and ten, feeling he was somehow duty bound to ensure the others went inside theirs first. He owed these people so much.

Watching their backs was the least he could do.

Chapter Two

Watching Vann from the corner of his eye was Kip's specialty. He was a pro at it and had learnt to behave that way ever since he'd stepped foot on the soil at Crossways for the first time. Back then he'd had his mother to look after, but then Vann had come along and Kip had him to think of too. Until his mother was —

No. I won't go there. Not at the moment.

He wanted to remain alert to anything his Dom might want of him, always. Sensitive to Vann's needs, he waited for what he knew was to come once Vann had swiped their key card down the slot. The door clicked open and Vann stepped inside, Kip close at his heels. Even though Dillon had been in there already, Vann would check the room himself — closets, the bathroom, beneath the bed. Everywhere.

"*Sit,*" Vann ordered.

Kip sat on the bed, bowed his head and clutched his open Taser bag. He had no qualms about using the weapon. People thought him meek and mild, but if they knew the feisty spirit that lived inside him, they'd soon think again. He hadn't always lived at Crossways. He'd been lucky to experience life outside its constricting confines, and although his years at the compound had somewhat deadened his soul, he'd never doubted that he'd escape one day. Being with Vann had gotten Kip through, helped to keep insanity at bay. And there had been times Kip had thought he might go mad—mad with the need to get the pack to turn on Bennett and give him the same medicine he dished out to others. That he'd dished out to Kip's mother.

Don't think about that.

Instead, he went back to his previous musings about the Taser. If wielding such a dangerous item meant saving Vann, he'd do it—to save himself too. He didn't want to have Vann go through losing him. He didn't think the man could bear life without him. Vann's thoughts had told him as much, especially when he'd been worrying that the plane would crash. Kip had purposely stared out of the window, keeping his own thoughts serene and happy so Vann would pick up on them and they'd help to calm him. Many a lonely night at Crossways had seen them talking to one another in their heads, getting close in mind when they couldn't in body. And that had been one of the reasons Kip had wanted to escape that place so badly. To be allowed to touch and speak to Vann without fear of being caught and punished.

Not only that, but to seek help, to find someone who believed them about Bennett and who would help to bring him down. It turned out Bennett had brought himself down...

Kip shook his head to get rid of the thoughts. He kept an eye on Vann covertly, his heart bursting with love so Vann would feel it. At the moment, from what

Kip could feel, Vann was on the edge, just about ready to blow a gasket through fear, panic and uncertainty. Kip hated for Vann to feel that way, but he knew it would take years — possibly their lifetime together — for Vann to accept and believe in freedom.

Kip had been surprised Vann had coped with their journey on foot from one side of Texas to the other. He'd expected him to jump at every little thing, each new experience too much in a short space of time. But he'd managed well enough, and here they were, in a hotel room after riding on a plane.

How times changed.

Used to Crossways living, Vann lifted things one after the other — lamps, the phone, even the comfortable-looking chair in the corner. He opened drawers then took off his shoes to stand on the bed and inspect the light fitting, unscrewing it to peer inside at the wires. He vanished into the bathroom then returned, pacing at the foot of the bed, resting his finger across his bottom lip. Nothing seemed to contain listening devices or cameras — and Vann knew all about those, having found so many when he'd done the same kind of inspection at Crossways.

It came naturally to Vann — after all, it had been a part of his daily life.

Kip coughed quietly. Vann stopped pacing and gave Kip his attention. Kip smiled. Vann returned it and his handsome face lightened Kip's heart. He'd swear it had turned over. How would he have got through this without Vann — got through his adulthood so far, since Bennett had killed Kip's mother? Their recent escape from Crossways had been fraught with danger. It was a miracle they'd slipped past the guards — a miracle because the two on duty had stolen a bottle of Bennett's rum and had gotten themselves as drunk as lords. They'd been slumped against the wall, on their asses instead of their feet, fast asleep. The empty bottle wedged between them had been the accusatory, pointing finger, screaming about how they'd gotten into such a state.

Kip wondered what the guards punishment had been when they had been found like that, but he needn't have bothered. He knew full well what would have happened. Bennett would have ordered that the guards be ripped to shreds by his loyal shifters—shifters Vann reckoned were only loyal because they were scared out of their wits.

"It'll be all right, Sir. No need to think bad thoughts." Kip took hold of Vann's hand. He kissed the back of it, letting his lips linger. *"We're safe with these Highgate people. I feel it. Knew it as soon as I saw them in the woods after we first met Louie and Jace."*

Jace was someone Vann had yet to know. Time hadn't been on their side but, God willing, when they returned to Highgate, maybe Vann and Jace could catch up on all the years they'd been forced to spend apart. Vann had confided in Kip, telling him, once they'd mated and could hear each other's thoughts, how he longed to escape and find his brother so they could return and free the rest of the pack. Kip could have wondered how Vann felt returning here without Jace, but he didn't have to. He sensed the tinge of sorrow inside Vann, where his dream of two brothers joining in battle hadn't come to fruition. That sorrow was eclipsed by a stronger emotion, though—relief that Jace would never have to see Crossways, would never be put in danger there.

"I know we're safe with them."

Vann's words startled Kip out of his musings.

"But it's so difficult to shake off how we've always had to live," Vann continued. "I know how to trust" — he smiled — "as do you. We trust my parents, my sister, and each other. But trusting strangers? All right, they're good strangers and I've scented no animosity from them since we established who we are, but…"

"I understand, but I do think they're truly on our side. Otherwise, why would we be here?" Kip smiled again. "Why would they have spent so much money getting their team across the state? People don't usually throw cash about, you know. And we met Alpha Newart. There's no way he would allow us to go with the Highgate men if he thought they posed a threat."

"I keep forgetting he gave his consent for this. But us having been shielded from pack life outside Crossways — hell, Alpha Newart may as well be just as much a stranger as anyone else."

"Please would you stop that, Sir — tormenting yourself? Forgive me if I'm speaking out of turn, but Alpha Newart is the equivalent of our king. A good man."

"Kings can also be corrupt." Vann raised his hand then brought it down, thumping his thigh. "Shit, I don't think I'll ever fully trust anyone other than you, Mom, Dad and Terena."

The mention of Vann's sister had Kip wondering how she was faring without her brother. They were close, and Vann had hated leaving her behind. Finding out from Bennett when he'd been caught at Highgate that Vann's mother was ill from food poisoning — deliberate poisoning on Bennett's part — had been a particularly harsh blow. But if Vann was going out of his mind with worry about her, he was doing a good job of outwardly hiding it from Kip.

"Talk to me, Sir? Out loud? It's so good to be able to do that now. We forget we're not at Crossways half the time and chat inside our heads, but we don't have to now you've checked for devices. I love hearing your voice."

Vann plonked himself down on the bed beside Kip, and Kip sensed he was remembering how it had been in the past. To touch in public had been dangerous. They'd snatched hurried moments, and their true mating had occurred in the middle of the night after Bennett had consumed too much rum and had been snoring in his room.

The wine cellar had been the safest place—somewhere others didn't go, because it was cold and dark and harbored cobwebs and the spiders that had created them. Fucking in such a place wasn't Kip's idea of romantic—it wasn't a clean, homely venue—but it hadn't mattered. To Kip it had been a sumptuous hotel room. In his mind the damp walls were papered with glossy images of movie stars from a bygone age. The wooden pallets they'd made into a bed was a four-poster covered in a fluffy quilt made of velvet, matching curtains hanging all around, giving them the privacy they craved. The stench of mold was spring flowers, the first blooms of the season, their scent pretty and comforting.

To be alone on their journey across Texas was one of the highlights of Kip's life. Yes, it had been more like an arduous trek than a lazy, enjoyable walk in the park, but at least they'd had one another—and they'd finally been free. They might have slept rough, but they had been together. And at Highgate they'd shared a proper bed in the main pack house. All right, the walls hadn't been adorned with film stars, the quilt hadn't been velvet but it had felt just as soft. And now, here they were in a hotel room with an hour or so of quality time and Vann was worrying about the coming mission. That was understandable, but if Kip could take Vann's mind off it for just a moment, he'd be happy.

His mother had brought Kip up to be a gentleman, something she said his father had never been. To please Vann was Kip's main objective, and he'd do it as often as he could or die trying.

I might die trying too.

He shoved that thought away, focusing instead on how he could switch Vann's mood from fretful to happy. But Vann's thoughts leached into his head, corrupting Kip's and dominating his mind. Kip frowned. He could have shut the images out, but how could he fix things if he did that? Vann was feeling guilty about Kip's mother. She'd been killed after Bennett had forced her to mate with a lion shifter. How he'd found one to participate in such a thing Kip didn't know. Lion shifters were notorious for hiding out. They didn't have compounds, instead choosing to live among fulls as humans, their need to keep their shifter status a secret their top priority. Kip supposed there were warped and twisted people in all walks of life. Why would lions be any different? And to mix breeds like that? God Almighty, Bennett had been playing with fire.

Vann sighed, his mind going to the cubs that Kip's mother had birthed. Kip was twenty-two—his mother had had him when she'd been nineteen—and although she hadn't been old in human terms to have more children when she'd had the mixed-breed cubs, she'd been old for a shifter. She had been lucky that she hadn't died while in labor, but that was a moot point. She'd died anyway, after they'd been born and at Bennett's order. He'd gotten what he'd wanted, so she'd been surplus to requirements. And she might have escaped, opened her mouth and let the world know what Bennett had made her do. There was no way he'd have allowed that.

Kip had accepted her death as gracefully as she would have expected him to. It didn't mean he wasn't hurting—he was—but he forced himself to stay positive in her memory. She'd have hated him to sink into grief so deep he couldn't find his way out.

Vann's mind drifted, bringing an image of Vann's father into Kip's head. Kip had known that would come next. It was inevitable. Vann's father, Aaron, and Kip's mother were linked in the most horrific of ways. Aaron was a scientist, and Bennett had made him perform experiments prior to the wolf-lion mating. Aaron had discovered that although cats and dogs wouldn't ordinarily produce viable fetuses, wolves and lions would. Aaron could have said what Bennett wanted wasn't possible, but the man had been afraid of Bennett as much as they all were at Crossways. And Bennett had had a knack of spotting a lie a mile off. Aaron hadn't taken the risk.

Kip didn't often speak without permission, but this time it was warranted. They were, as far as he was concerned, still in a conversation he'd been given consent to engage in. "I don't blame your father, Sir. You know that, so why should you feel bad for what he's done? If he could turn back the clock, he would."

"I know, but… Fuck, I can't get it all out of my head. It keeps coming back after I think it's gone. It'll always be there."

"Maybe Sergeant will know how to help you put it all to rest. Maybe this mission will help. Maybe I can. Sir, I hate to see you like this. Please let me make it better?"

Vann pulled Kip to his side, holding him there with his arm around his back. The contact was welcome—

so much that Kip sagged against him. Vann didn't offer anything more verbally, and Kip decided to give him time. His mate always tended to stew on something for a while then suddenly snap out of it, as though he couldn't bear to think anymore. Kip would then take over, kissing Vann senseless so nothing danced in his head except for erotic images of them together.

While he waited for Vann to pull out of his fugue, Kip sorted through his own worries. How would Vann feel when he stepped foot on Crossways again? He'd been incarcerated there his whole life, wishing every day that he could escape. Then he had, and now they were going back. It sounded insane, their return to such a nasty place, but Vann wasn't the kind of man to leave his family and the rest of the pack to suffer under Wickland's rule.

This is all such a horrible, tragic mess.

Vann got up. He went to the window and peered out. "When you arrived at Crossways, it was the best day of my life. Tell me about it again."

Kip smiled, remembering how frightened he'd been. "Again? All right. Bennett grabbed me and Mom off the street. We hadn't belonged to a pack since leaving my dad, living as fulls and hiding who and what we really were. At first, I thought Dad had found us, but Bennett had just guessed lucky that we were shifters and his use for Mom was quickly made apparent on the car journey to Crossways."

Kip shivered at the memory. Vann tended to ask him to repeat what Kip had already told him because he said it had given him light at the end of the tunnel when they'd been at Crossways. Perhaps it was a habit, wanting to know the story remained consistent with every telling. Kip indulged him, understanding that Bennett had done the same to Vann all his life and that such a procedure was natural for him.

"You were the first shifter I saw on our arrival, and I instantly fell for you, big man, Sir. The rest is history… Something we must pick over in the future when we have more time to reminisce."

"I love that memory. As you know, I fell hard for you that day too and I've been falling harder every day since."

"I love you so much, Sir."

"I know that."

"Won't you let me make everything go away? We have a little while before we have to meet Dillon and the others for dinner."

"Only if you really want to. You must be tired. We walked a long way. We ought to rest up as much as we can."

"I can handle whatever you want to dish out, Sir. And I'm not tired. I'll sleep when I'm dead. And at the moment, I'd rather be fucked by you."

Chapter Three

Vann should have felt too tired, too wired up to fuck, but Christ, Kip always knew exactly what he needed and when.

"Get your clothes off," Vann said, rising to go and stand with his back to the wall opposite the foot of the bed. "And take them off slowly. We've always been so rushed in the past. And I'll give talking out loud a go. Because you want that, don't you?" He paused. "Permission to speak throughout this scene."

"Yes, Sir. I want that. I've always wanted that."

It seemed alien to say the words instead of thinking them. He'd have to make a conscious effort not to slip into thought. His time with Kip was always silent, even grunts and moans were held back. What would it be like to let them loose? And spanking—they'd wanted to try it, but the sound of slaps on bare skin were a risk they hadn't dared take. Pack members could have heard it and come along to investigate. And if it had been anyone other than those well under Bennett's thumb, maybe they'd have got away with it, but the risk had been too great to take.

Things were going to be different from now on, but it would take a while to get used to it. Switching from one kind of lifestyle to another wouldn't be something either of them could do at the drop of a hat. Like Sergeant asking Vann to just call him Sergeant and not sir. It felt wrong somehow, as though he'd get punished for it.

Don't think of all that, not when you have special time with Kip.

Kip stood and bowed his head. Vann almost asked him to lift it so he could see his face but resisted. His lover was more comfortable showing complete submission, and although that turned Vann on, he couldn't help but wish that sometimes Kip would make eye contact without being told to. He loved looking into Kip's eyes, reading the wealth of information there — the emotions, the love.

Kip seemed distracted. Vann connected with him mentally to see whether something was wrong. All he saw inside his head, and felt in his heart, was a galaxy. What did that mean?

"One day, Sir, would you fuck me beneath the stars? Just once, that's all I want."

Vann swallowed. So the galaxy was Kip thinking of stars and infinity — of them being together forever?

"We can do that, yes," Vann said. The idea of outside sex... *Fucking hot.*

"Thank you, Sir."

Tugging his T-shirt up, Kip revealed his slender belly then his chest. His small pink nipples stood out, the usually hairless skin just starting to show signs of needing to be waxed again. He had a trail of curls going from his navel and down, though. Vann loved pressing his cheek to it, the rough yet soft fuzz tickling his skin. Once, he'd done that for a whole five minutes, the pair of them wedged behind a stack of crates in the storage room. That moment had seemed never-ending, yet at the same time it hadn't been long enough. Vann could lose himself in Kip and never get lost.

He thought of what was under the rest of Kip's clothing. Vann's cock hardened.

Kip dropped the T-shirt onto the bed. He undid his borrowed belt that held up slightly too big jeans then pulled it from the waistband loops. And, God, he raised his head. Stared directly at Vann.

"Sir?"

"Yes."

That was all Vann had needed to say for Kip to hold the belt out. Vann pushed off the wall. He took the leather strap. Went back to his former position. Kip looked down at the carpet while removing the jeans, then toed off the shoes and socks before sweeping it all away with his foot. There was no underwear—neither of them had wanted to borrow something so intimate—and there was Kip, naked and so very wanted.

His flaccid cock wouldn't come to life until Vann ordered Kip to let his lust be on display. Kip's amazing self-control was nothing short of staggering. Vann supposed their time together had seen to that, with Kip keeping a rein on his thoughts to the point that any reaction from his body was stopped before a natural effect could take place. He didn't understand how it worked, because when Vann was turned on, nothing could stop his dick getting hard.

"How do you do that?" Vann asked.

"Do what, Sir?"

"Not get hard when—" He stopped to think about what he was going to say—*when you're about to have sex…when you're turned on?*

Was Kip even turned on? Was the act of getting undressed in front of Vann, knowing they were about to fuck, not thrilling? They were wired differently, he knew that, but… He mentally reached out but felt and sensed nothing from Kip—nothing except the need to please.

"I don't know, Sir, but there are certain things you do, certain things you say, *then* I get hard. I've had to hide how I feel, don't forget. Maybe the idea of being caught by someone at Crossways triggered something in my mind. I just knew that unless I felt completely safe, I couldn't… Being seen with a hard cock—it would have given everything away and Bennett would have made sure we never saw one another again."

"No one is here to stop us now. To see us." *Am I trying to convince him or myself?* "And if they do see us, so what?"

Kip smiled, shrugged. *So what.* "Are you going to hit me with that belt, Sir?"

"Yes."

Kip's cock jumped.

Vann wanted to see when Kip's cock hardened, to get to know what set him off. "I'm going to slap that pretty little ass of yours while you're bending over the bed."

There. Kip's dick expanded, lengthened—not fully erect but…

"And I'm going to enjoy seeing how pink it gets."

More dick reaction.

"And I'm going to love hearing you cry out, begging me to do it again and again."

"You see, Sir? See what you've done?" Kip looked up at him, staring for a few seconds then lowering his head once more.

"Oh, I see it all right. Your hard cock, the way it's standing up, almost touching your belly." Vann hesitated, wishing he could give Kip several instructions at once, thinking they needed to hurry then realizing they didn't. "Touch it."

Kip immediately wrapped his fingers around his erection, and Vann knew the weightiness of it, how it felt against his palm. Kip mentally opened up and transferred his emotions, thinking something Vann would never have imagined Kip would want.

"So you want to jerk off at the *window*?" Vann widened his eyes. He tried to come to terms with that. His Kip, needing to…expose himself?

"Yes, Sir. I want the risk of being seen. I want the freedom of it—the freedom of choice. If I *am* seen, it doesn't mean death or separation from you now, just a shocked viewer at the least and a tap on the wrist from the police if we're reported at the most. But we'll be careful, won't we, Sir? Just being at the window will be enough—the thought, the idea of being caught will be enough. I don't have to show…all of me to whoever might be outside."

The scenario flashed through Vann's mind, and he had to admit that fuck, it was a turn-on. For someone to catch sight of Kip like that, and Vann knowing Kip was his, that whoever watched couldn't have him…

"How much do you want this?" Vann asked.

"Can't you feel it? Don't you know, Sir?"

Vann's desire grew. "Get over to the window, damn it."

Kip walked across the room, his body movements lithe, precise, fluid. Jeez, Vann loved him.

"That's it. Stand there—right there. They'll only be able to see your face, your chest, but when you jerk off…" Vann coughed. "They'll see the top of your arm moving. They'll know exactly what you're doing. Oh, God, do it. Do it now."

Vann remained with his back pressed to the wall. No way could he go over there with Kip at the moment. If he did, he'd fuck him in the ass seven ways to Sunday.

Kip started up a slow rhythm, staring down at…what, a car park? The street? Vann's mind was scrambled and he couldn't recall what their window faced.

"What's out there?" Vann demanded.

"The road outside the airport, Sir. The cabs. People…"

"Christ Almighty. Tell me about the people. What are they doing?" Vann resisted taking his own cock in hand.

"Waiting for cabs, Sir. Talking." Kip worked himself faster. "Oh! Someone's turned to stare at the hotel."

"Shit." This was hot—hotter than Vann thought it should be. The risk, the freedom—it was going to get to him if he didn't rein in his emotions. "Man or woman?"

"Man. He's… I think he's seen me." Kip gripped the sill with his free hand. His fingers bent at the middle knuckles, and he pressed the tips against the wood, the skin going whiter from the pressure.

"You're almost there?" Vann could have kicked himself for slipping into the old habit. He repeated himself aloud, voice cracked.

"Yes, Sir, this is… Please…"

The vision of the belt flew through Vann's mind, sent to him from Kip. He strode over to the window, standing close behind Kip—close enough that Kip's elbow jabbed him in the stomach as he played with his cock. The man outside stood on the path, staring up at their window, his eyebrows raised. For a second or two Vann's instinct was to drag Kip away. That guy could be anyone, someone sent to find them, to follow them. But his face showed his surprise and intrigue, not recognition.

He wasn't someone Vann found attractive — and Kip didn't either, judging by Kip's thoughts and feelings. But that didn't matter. It was just knowing the man was watching that did the trick. Vann's stomach rolled over, and for a second or two he forgot the rules in their new life. Possibly because they could still get into trouble if they were caught, just in a different way.

"Ah, jeez, he knows what you're doing," Vann said. "How does that make you feel?"

"Alive, Sir. Like I can do anything I want, within reason."

Vann stepped back to give himself room to use the belt but to also give Kip his moment — just Kip and the watching stranger. Vann would stay in the background, giving Kip his other dream.

A whipping.

"Prepare yourself," Vann warned.

Instead of tensing his back muscles, Kip bent over a little, jutting his ass out. He spread his legs, balls swaying with his movements on his dick. The sight was beautiful, and Vann grew hornier. Would he last through the scene without coming too soon? Their former trysts had been over so fast that he hadn't needed to master the art of control. Now, he fought to hold off his orgasm, balancing on an edge he'd never stood on before.

"I'm going to use the belt now," he said.

"Please, Sir. Yes, please." Kip masturbated faster, harder, stuck his ass out farther.

Vann held the buckle then wrapped some of the belt around his hand, leaving enough length that would give Kip the smack he needed but not hurt too much. This was their first time doing something like this. Previously, fantasies were all they'd had. They'd shared thoughts about how it might feel, and to be honest, Vann had told himself they'd never get the opportunity to find out. Getting away from Crossways had seemed unattainable. And imagining was nothing like the real thing, as Vann was quickly finding out. The feel of the belt, the squeeze of it in his hand... Man, what would using it be like if his cock throbbed the way it was just by him preparing to strike? Would he come where he stood?

Before his need for release overtook him, Vann concentrated on what he was about to do. He'd tested this out on himself before, lightly striking then progressing to using more force. He had some idea of how hard he should hit, but doing it to someone else might be different. Vann had felt pain—the kind he didn't want. How would it feel for Kip, who wanted it to hurt? How much hurt did Kip need to satisfy his craving?

"Just do it, Sir. However hard you want. I need... That man's still staring and I..." Kip's knees gave way and he groaned, slowing his speed a little.

"Do *not* come," Vann ordered, realizing things might have gone too fast already. "Not until I give you permission."

Kip slowed his jerks.

Vann positioned himself side-on then raised the belt, worried he'd make a mess of this but wanting to hurry so that Kip got what he was desperate for. Vann brought the belt down in an arc. The sound of it smacking into the flesh of Kip's ass was loud—louder than Vann had expected. Kip jolted his pelvis forward, almost colliding into the wall below the window. Kip moaned then sighed in pleasure.

Vann struck him again, harder this time, and watched in fascination as a pink welt blossomed on his skin.

"Oh! Sir... More, please?"

Vann obliged, going for one last bite of leather on ass cheek, not wanting to overwhelm Kip for his first time being flogged. The crack of sound had Vann's balls drawing up, and he sucked in a sharp breath to focus on not coming.

"Ah! Enough, Sir." Kip looked over his shoulder at Vann. "Come here. Please?"

Vann let the belt unwind from his hand. He let it go and it fell to the floor, the buckle thudding. He stepped over it, eager to get to the window, to get closer to Kip. Vann stared through the glass. The man had gone to sit on a bench, one arm braced on the back, his free hand up against his forehead, as though he was shielding his eyes from the waning sun.

"That's not for the sun," Vann said. "He's done that to get a better look at you. See his face? The way he's trying to keep a neutral expression? He doesn't want anyone else to know what he's doing, watching a man jerking off. But he likes it all right. Yeah, he likes seeing my mate fucking himself."

"Oh, Sir...what you said—that's what I meant earlier. Certain things you say, the way you say them... I can't... Sir, please may I come?"

"No."

Kip whimpered, his hand working so furiously Vann was amazed his sub could keep that speed up without spurting spunk all over the wall.

"You see how he's sitting? He's got a hard dick, that man." Vann breathed heavily. "He's as hard as rock and wishes he could jab your ass with his dick. He wants my mate—but he can't have him. No, you're mine, and only I'm allowed in your ass."

Vann brushed his lips down the side of Kip's neck. He rested his hand on Kip's stomach, covering Kip's jerk-off hand with his other. He closed his eyes.

"How does your ass feel? Tell me."

"Hot. So hot, Sir. And sore but in a good way."

"So you liked it then?"

"I loved it."

"Good, but maybe you'll love my cock in your ass more. Maybe you'll love me fucking you from behind, knowing that guy can see us."

"I will, Sir. Oh, God, I will."

"Then I'll get the lube."

Chapter Four

Kip held his breath. This was sublime. Together like this, without any worries apart from that man down there calling the cops... He wished they'd been able to do this long ago, but there was no sense in wallowing in the past. Not when nothing could be changed. They'd done the best they could in the circumstances, and although it had never been enough as he'd always needed more, he'd been content.

He waited for the cold touch of gel. Where Vann had gotten lube from he didn't know, but he sure as hell wasn't about to query it now. His dick had gone numb from jerking off but he just needed permission from Vann to come and all feeling would return. He'd shut off his need, although it had been difficult what with the man outside still enjoying the free show and Vann behind him, close enough for Kip to feel his body heat but not *close enough*. Kip wanted skin on skin, for Vann to press his body against his, to be made to feel whole. He wanted to cry out, to express himself by using his voice instead of biting his tongue and clamping his lips shut.

This... What they were doing... It could have been seen as sordid, for him to want a stranger to ogle him. And perhaps it could also have been seen as Kip being disloyal to Vann. Kip wanting more than Vann, another partner. But it wasn't like that. The guy on the bench was nothing more than a symbol of what Kip and Vann had never had—freedom to be with one another without fear of being caught by Bennett or his men. To be able to say, without words, 'Hey, we're together, we love each other', was amazing.

The cold lube he'd been anticipating came, slathered down his ass crack then swirled around his hole. He sighed loudly, holding back a groan then letting it out when he remembered he could make whatever noise he liked now. Vann massaged his hole, circling the pucker. Kip clenched his cheeks on instinct, trapping Vann's fingers, then he relaxed as the fluid warmed.

"I heard what you thought," Vann said, "and I'd never think you'd want another man. I understand why you need this."

Vann continued circling a fingertip around Kip's entrance. The feeling in Kip's cock came back, a great smack of lust that had him dragging in a deep breath.

"Oh, Sir! I need..."

"I know what you need."

Vann slid a fingertip inside, Kip's rim clamping it tight. Vann eased in some more then added another, scissoring to expand the opening. Kip gave in to it, bearing down so pain didn't have a mind to rip through him. Vann pushed in then pulled out, repeating the motion until, when he brushed Kip's sweet spot, Kip let out a ragged moan. How had they fucked in silence for so long? How had they managed to get intimate for such a short amount of time and be fulfilled?

We weren't. Not really. I realize that now. And oh, Vann can really be who he's meant to be now. My Master. I can't wait to see what's in store for us in the future. I want him to do whatever he wants. I want him to do it right now.

Taking his fingers out then fingering the pucker of muscle, Vann whispered, "You're ready."

Kip nodded, unable to respond because damn, he was almost there. If he didn't focus on waiting, on obeying his Master, he'd come.

Vann pressed the end of his cock to Kip's hole. Kip bent a bit more at the waist, shoving his ass back so that Vann's tip got sucked inside. The stretch—God, the stretch was like nothing else, all wicked heat and the searing longing to be stretched even more.

Reading Kip's emotions, Vann slid in fully, keeping still when he was in up to his balls. Kip held his breath, loving the sensation of being filled to capacity. He relaxed some more, slowing down on his own cock. It throbbed in time with the pulsing heat in his ass—Vann's cock, Vann just as greedy for release as Kip was.

Withdrawing slowly, Vann toyed with Kip's nipples, twisting them so sharp pains shot from there outwards, springing goosebumps on Kip's skin. Then Vann thrust in, and Kip cried out, jerking himself faster, gripping the sill harder.

"He's watching us both now," Vann said, pumping in and out of his ass with no mercy. "And he knows you're mine and I'm yours. I bet he can see it on our faces—the love, the need. And he wants it for himself but"—Vann pushed in, a fierce thrust—"he can't have it. Not with you. Not with me." He sped up, his cock gliding easily with the lube. "Never, because we belong to each other."

"Yes, Sir. Yes. Oh, I'm…"

"Come. Come all over my damn fingers so I can lick it off after." Vann lowered one hand from a nipple. He cupped his palm over the end of Kip's dick. "Fuck yourself. Go on, fuck yourself hard."

Kip needed no more encouragement. He let his mind receive all the messages his body threw at it.

Touch me. Fuck me. You feel so good against me, Sir.

If Vann told him to hold back again now, Kip would fail. It was too late for that. Cum seemed to swirl in his balls before shooting up his cock. His dick veins pulsed on his palm, his ass was on fire from the rapid friction and his heart... His heart was at one with his mate's.

Everything shattered in him, an explosion of pleasure and love that made him close his eyes and tip his head back to lean on Vann's collarbone. Spunk jetted out of him. Kip's fingertips on the sill ached, but he couldn't let go. Not yet, not until it was over. His legs almost gave out on him, and for the first time he keened so loudly it brought joy — the kind he'd always wanted to experience but never could.

"We're fucking free, Sir."

Vann grunted — what a welcome sound — and emptied his balls into Kip's spasming ass. Kip opened his eyes to see that the guy outside had gone. It didn't matter. He'd served his purpose, and now Kip could move on from the constraints of their past and embrace a bright new future.

"*I love you!*" Vann rammed in and out as his cock pulsed and he released the last of his cum.

"I love you too, Sir," Kip managed, out of breath, his chest tight, his legs weaker.

Vann took his hand away from Kip's cock. "Lick," he ordered.

Kip opened his mouth to suck in a cum-soaked finger. He'd done this before, lapped Vann's stomach clean when they'd fucked in closets or in shadowy corners at Crossways, but his cum had never tasted this good. Liberty infused it with goodness, giving it a sweeter tang. He closed his eyes again and sagged against Vann, moaning around the finger.

Vann pulled his finger out, and Kip opened his eyes to watch him lick the rest off. Kip took in all the things he was feeling—throbbing ass and cock, heart thumping hard, neck vein flickering. And happiness so great he forgot everything for a few seconds.

As though knowing he'd forgotten their purpose here, his brain gave him a reminder. The reason they were in the hotel came stomping back. A respite, that's all their fuck had been. Yet it hadn't, not really. It was an awakening, something that had pushed them to the next level. There were so many more levels they had to reach, and once they'd been on the mission, Kip couldn't wait to get to them all. No more hiding. No more pretending they didn't know each other. Wherever they ended up living, hopefully they could do as they pleased, touching, holding hands, maybe a sweet kiss without fear.

"It'll be great, won't it?" Vann murmured, his breath hot on Kip's neck. "To just be us."

"Yes, Sir."

Vann pulled his softening cock out. He turned Kip around to face him then hugged him close. Kip wrapped his arms around Vann's waist, pushing his cheek to his chest. The warmth from his skin seeped into Kip. They stood that way for what seemed like forever, Kip reveling in there being no particular hurry. The time did cross Vann's mind, though, only fleeting but there, and it snatched Kip out of his blissful cocoon and into the present.

"We need to shower. Think about the mission. Talk about it," Vann said. "I don't want to stop what we're doing, but we can't let Dillon and the others down."

Kip nodded and followed Vann after he'd broken their embrace to head toward the bathroom. They shared the tub, washing each other in silence at first. Kip marveled at the fact they could do this, how something that came so easily to others—taken for granted perhaps—had been a pipe dream to them.

"I didn't think," Kip whispered, "that we'd…" He smoothed his hands up Vann's chest, bubbles disguising his fingers. "This feels like a dream, Sir."

Except he knew it wasn't. The water was hot and real, the soapsuds fluffy and soft, their bodies close, bellies touching. And now, lips touching, Vann kissing him with passion, as though he never wanted to let Kip go.

"Stay safe," Vann thought. *"Never put yourself in danger on this mission. You're my life and I—"*

"We'll be fine, Sir. Just fine."

The water chilled a fraction, snatching away their special moment. Kip helped the shower stream wash away the lather on Vann's body, swiping the bubbles until only suspicions of it clung to the hairs around Vann's cock. Vann returned the gesture then switched the shower off. They stepped out of the tub then dried without speaking, the towel an abrasion on Kip's sore ass cheek.

"Is it too sore?" Vann asked. "Will it hurt to put clothes on?"

"It'll be okay, Sir." Kip studied the floor tiles. "And if it isn't, then it'll soon heal when I shift. That's the sad part about being a wolf. Every time I have a smacked ass and want it to hurt for a week, the wolf in me will demand I shift and take away the pain."

Vann shivered, and if Kip couldn't read Vann's mind he'd think he was cold. But no, that had been a shiver of desire, the anticipation of the things to come. The toys they could use, the hours they could spend indulging in sex.

"I can't wait, Sir. Can you?"

"No, but we have to. One more hurdle and we can start living properly." Vann reached out to take a corner of Kip's towel. He used it to dry his cheeks then pushed up under Kip's chin so their gazes met. "A few hours and it will all be over. God, how I wish it was over already. What we have to do is dangerous and—"

"I know, Sir. And we'll get through it like we always do."

"Together."

Kip nodded. "Permission to hug you, Sir?"

Vann held his arms out, and Kip walked into them. He'd never get tired of this. Vann's hugs erased every bad thing, replacing it with goodness, security and the knowledge that their mating had been the best thing to happen to Kip.

"I love you, Sir. So much."

Vann didn't answer. Instead, he squeezed Kip tighter and sent his love flying, right into Kip's chest. Kip was full of it—Vann's and his own—and it just about knocked him flat on his ass. How could so much love exist between two people? How would it be possible to feel more as their life went on?

"Because our hearts will grow bigger," Vann said. "And they'll have to, because I have so much more love to show you. It's just waiting to come out. I stored it for the whole time we were together at

Crossways. Dreams, hugs, kisses—so many things I wanted to do spontaneously and couldn't. Every time I thought of them, I added them to the 'later' pile. You have quite a cache to enjoy."

Kip closed his eyes, never wanting this moment to end. He soaked everything in. The plop of water dripping off the showerhead and into the tub. Vann's steady breathing. The warmth their bodies generated. The scent of lemons and jasmine from the soap. The puddle of water at Kip's feet. Their towels slipping off. Bodies pressing closer together. The damp curls on Vann's chest a pillow for Kip's cheek.

Perfect. So perfect.

"We need to get ready," Vann said.

The spell was broken. Kip sighed, moving away so Vann could leave the bathroom. Kip dipped his head, trailing him to the bed. He sat without being told to, sensing that was what Vann wanted. And as much as he loathed pushing aside the contentment, the happiness, Kip switched his mind to the mission while Vann dressed.

"There are things we need to talk about before we go down to the dining room." Vann cleared his throat. "And please get dressed."

Kip obeyed.

"We're to stick together as much as possible," Vann went on. "No being separated unless it's absolutely necessary. I want to know where you are at all times. To be able to see you."

"I understand, Sir, but we have our thoughts. You'll know I'm safe when I speak to you that way if we get parted."

"It's not the same." Vann went to the window. Snapped the curtains closed as though the memory of what they'd done there was a distraction. "We're a team."

Kip nodded, fully dressed now. He attempted to tie the laces on his shoes, fingers shaking, him fumbling and cursing himself for showing fear.

I'm not afraid. I can't be afraid. Vann mustn't know I'm worried.

"Dillon knows what he's doing," Kip said. "He has everything mapped out."

"But not all eventualities. He doesn't know Wickland. Or any of Wickland's men. Yeah, he's studied the layout at Crossways, but it's never the same as actually being there. Things can go wrong."

"They won't."

"How can you be so sure?"

I wasn't sure, but I am now. Something's clicked inside me, some kind of knowledge and... "Because I just know, Sir. I can't explain it, but this is the last leg for us. We release the pack then move on. Put the past firmly behind us. We have to."

"It might not be that easy. The memories, the times we—"

"Forgive me for interrupting, Sir, but I know how to shut things off. It's like they don't exist anymore when I do it. I'll teach you how to do the same."

Vann turned from the window. "Look at me."

Kip raised his head, stared into Vann's eyes.

"What if I can't learn, Kip? What if the past won't fuck off?"

"It will. You'll get through this, Sir. I'll make sure of it."

Chapter Five

Dinner passed all too quickly. Although Vann wanted to get things over and done with at Crossways, he was afraid of returning there. It might seem inconceivable to some that a big man like himself would feel fear, but he did. He was part human, after all, and had feelings like anyone else. Conditioned as he'd been all his life to toe the line, a huge part of him still had the desire to do that. Every aspect regarding 'do as you're told' was so ingrained, set deep inside him, that he wondered if he'd ever shake it free. With Bennett incarcerated, the threat should have been gone—if Wickland wasn't around. He was the stumbling block.

The man who may well fuck this whole mission up.

The one who might capture Vann and Kip, catch the Highgate men, ensuring their lives would go back to how they were before. Providing they weren't killed for leaving Crossways in the first place. And the cover story that had been concocted for when Vann and Kip met up with Wickland again. If things went wrong, and Wickland believed Vann, it meant Vann's life would be spared and Kip's wouldn't. Vann hadn't been happy about that, but Dillon had assured him everything would go well, that he knew what he was doing.

While the Highgate group had eaten, Vann had gone over the crude plans he'd drawn of Crossways again so everyone was familiar with the layout. It was imperative the whole group knew exactly where to go and when. One wrong move and shit would start flying. Dillon had chosen a private dining room—he'd thought of everything, it seemed—and they'd been able to talk freely once they'd ensured no listening devices or cameras were in place. Dillon had mentioned that their scouring of the private room might appear over the top, but he'd been in situations where information had been leaked and enemies had discovered his whereabouts, planting spyware. Vann knew all about that shit.

"So," Dillon said, pushing his plate to one side, "describe Wickland. We need to be aware of exactly who he is in case your part of the mission fails. Any distinguishing marks that would set him apart from everyone else? We don't want to Taser anyone who doesn't deserve it." He paused. "And damn, not knowing who is good and who is bad there puts pressure on us." He sighed. "Still, it's something we can't change, so I suggest we don't stress over it."

Vann didn't even know who was good or bad. Except for his family and a few others, everyone else had seemed to fit quite snugly into Bennett's pocket. Then again, they'd had no choice. It was obey or die, simple as that.

Better the devil you know…

He took a deep breath before answering. Bringing Wickland's face to mind, he shivered. The image wasn't the nicest thing he'd had to study. The thought of looking into those eyes again gave him the goddamn creeps, but he had to do it to save the Crossways pack.

"Yeah, he's easy to spot. Think Bennett but a little taller—maybe six-five. Dark, shaved hair. You can see his scalp. His eyes are blue, but a light color that borders on white. Fucking—excuse my language—eerie. And they bulge, like when someone's angry. Red rimmed too. And he's got this weird thing going on with his skin, like he's scarred on both cheeks but I think it might be from having acne years ago. Or maybe he got into a fight, I don't know." Vann shivered again. "But the most distinguishing thing is he has a cleft in his chin, a deep one, and in the middle of that is a large mole."

Dillon narrowed his eyes. Maybe he was visualizing the man in his head, or maybe he was already thinking about his next question. Whatever he was doing, Vann got the sense Dillon had several contingency plans stored in that brain of his and that the Highgate group would all get out of the mission alive with Dillon running the show.

I have to believe that. The alternative... No, I won't go there. Kip may pick up on my fear and I can't stand that.

"Where does he hang out?" Dillon asked, pushing the Crossways drawing into the center of the table so everyone could see.

"There." Vann pointed to a study just off the main foyer. "He calls it his control room. His job, before Bennett got caught, was the same as yours. Head of Security. So he has monitors that show all directions of the compound. He stays up late into the night, so there'll be no worries about speaking to him when we arrive. But that study... I hate the damn thing. It brings back horrible memories."

"So you've been in there?" Dillon took a sip of water, eyeing Vann over the glass rim.

"Once. Almost got caught. Wickland had gone to speak to the guards and hadn't locked the door. I wanted to see where the cameras were trained so me and Kip would know where we could get out without being seen." That time had had him fraught with anxiety. His blood had gone cold, his skin clammy. He'd asked himself what the hell he was playing at but there had been no choice if he and Kip were to get away successfully.

Dillon stroked his chin. "Yeah, you mentioned that. The way we get in is here, right?" He pressed a finger to a row of hedges that, with Vann's limited artistic ability, looked like puffy clouds. A kid's drawing.

"Yes, sir—er yes, Dillon. The cameras don't quite cover that whole area, so there's a gap between images that get transmitted. As the view on screen showed me, we'll have about twenty feet before we'd appear on either of those monitors."

"So we'll be seen regardless, because we'll be breaching that twenty feet." Dillon's face showed no expression.

"Which is why we agreed I'd enter the compound the proper way—via the front driveway." Vann squeezed Kip's hand under the table after feeling Kip's slight apprehension sliding through him. *It has to be this way, Kip. You know that. You may answer me."*

"I know, Sir, but it doesn't mean I have to like it."

"I don't either, but—"

"So you think you can pull it off without fucking it up?" Dillon asked.

"Yes." Vann smiled to project confidence to the group. To himself. *I have to pull it off. There's no other choice.*

Dillon stood. He rested his fingertips on the table, leaning onto them. "We all have our phones, our Tasers. Any one of us gets into trouble, hit the 'off' switch on your phones if you can. They're programmed this way because usually, when someone's caught, the captor switches off the phone. Works as a double alert."

Vann wondered where Dillon had got phones like that but didn't feel it was his place to ask. Dillon gave as little information as he could from what Vann had seen so far. He reckoned only Sergeant would know exactly who the real Dillon was.

"So." Dillon pushed off the table. He glanced at his watch. "Time to get going."

Vann's stomach churned. Excitement and nervousness squirreled through him. He let go of Kip's hand, hoping to God or whatever deity was out there that he'd get to hold it again after this. He rose, as did the rest of the group—except Kip.

"I can't give you orders from here on out." Vann didn't look at him. *"It won't work. As I said earlier, you need to drop our agreement at this point, like we did when we escaped."*

"Yes, Sir." Kip got up, fiddling with his Taser bag, although he didn't appear nervous at all.

"You okay?"

"Yes, Sir. You?"

"I'll get there."

Kip straightened his shoulders. It gave Vann confidence. If his little sub could go into this with the heart of a lion, so could Vann. He puffed out his chest, released a ragged sigh, and patted his Taser bag then his pocket to make sure his phone was still there. Everything was in order.

"The cabs should be waiting," Dillon said. "Paid for in advance. Good luck, and I'll see you on the flip side." He exited the room, leaving the door ajar.

The Highgate men followed, and Vann grabbed his alone moment with Kip to crush the slight man to him. He stroked his hair, loving the feel of Kip's cheek pressed to his chest, wishing things could have been so different.

"But if they were different, Sir, we never would have met."

"And people have suffered so that we met. I hate that."

"It is what it is, Sir. We can't change it now." Kip pulled away. *"Nor can we change the plan and the excuses we're going to give Wickland for why we left Crossways. Dillon will make sure we're not captured, that we're safe. Please don't worry about that anymore."*

Vann should have known Kip would pick up on his thoughts. Stupid of him to think otherwise when they were so connected. Even shutting his emotions off didn't keep Kip out sometimes.

Kip smiled. *"We have to go. We can't let the others down by stalling."*

"I love you."

"I know that, Sir."

Vann led the way out of the room and across the foyer. Kip walked by his side instead of slightly behind. It felt good to be equals, to walk as one. They made it to the line of cabs. Dillon stood by the back door of the first one, giving Vann a stern look. Vann blushed with the embarrassment of holding everyone up. Dillon's features then went blank again, but the admonishment emanating from him said Vann needed to buck up and stick to the plan. No deviating unless absolutely necessary.

Sometimes he wished there were thought links between all shifters so he could apologize without anyone else hearing. He hoped the expression on his face suitably conveyed how he felt. Dillon nodded, a curt dip of his head, then got into the cab. Vann, Kip and two shifters got into the last car. The others occupied two separate vehicles.

The journey was spent in silence, as they'd been ordered, so Vann stared through the window and examined his feelings. This return to Crossways was a tremendous leap from the one he'd thought would happen. To have a team on board rather than just him, Kip and, as he'd imagined, Jace, was more than he could have hoped for. He had doubts—who wouldn't?—but all in all, if they stuck to the plan and Wickland did as Vann anticipated, acting true to form, they'd have the pack free in no time.

As the cityscape turned from high-rises to empty spaces, Vann's uneasiness grew. He pushed intrusive thoughts of failure away—he *had* to remain positive.

"You'll make this work, Sir. I know you will."

"With you beside me, how can I fail?"

A glow of security blanketed Vann, and he sent loving thoughts to Kip, keeping back maudlin ones that he couldn't entertain right now. Like if things went wrong and Vann was killed, he'd wait for Kip in Heaven, counting the days until they could be together again.

"You didn't quite hide that thought, Sir."

Vann cursed himself.

"But I feel the same way." Kip patted Vann's leg. *"I'll wait for you too."*

There was no more time to reply. The cabs came to a stop on the lonely roadside. Vann's guts churned. This was it, the real start to their mission. Once those cars drove away, they were on their own.

No going back…

Everyone met on the verge and waited until the only indication that the vehicles had been there were specks of them on the horizon, back the way they'd come. The sun was setting, not long now until darkness descended.

"By the time we've run the remaining distance," Dillon said, "it'll be full dark. Vann's already mentioned that a lap of the compound by the guards is done every hour. Don't forget, they'll pass by our entry point *on* the hour. If we make decent time, as I hope we will, we'll be at our appointed place at eleven hundred hours." He looked at everyone in turn. "Next stage. Go."

Dillon took the lead, traipsing off toward a stand of trees. They had to strip there, stash their clothes beside trunks, put the phones in their Taser bags then shift. It was all done quickly and without talking or much effort, as though they'd been some kind of undercover team forever. Vann suspected the others had, and once again told himself not to fuck up. This group probably knew one another inside out—quirks, strengths, weaknesses—and had put a lot of trust in Vann and Kip by allowing them to join their band.

Although it felt good to be wolf, the pads of Vann's paws were goddamn sore again by the time they'd traveled maybe a mile. The rough ground wreaked havoc. For now, he'd just have to grin and bear it. The Taser bag strap scraped his tongue, and although the handle was short, the damn bag kept smacking into his front legs. It was an irritation he could have done without, but not taking the bags wasn't an option. Something else bothered him too. They were out in the open, easily spotted if a driver went past. All right, the wolves were quite a distance from the road, but if anyone had a sniper rifle, those on the mission would be easy pickings.

"Stop thinking like that, Sir, and just run. Focus on what's ahead but keep an eye on the road at the same time. Dillon will spot danger before we do, I know it."

Vann glanced across at Kip, who looked magical in his white coat. His strides were shorter than Vann's and therefore Kip would feel the journey more than the other, much bigger animals. Yet his determination was clear—there was a job to be done and they had to do it.

"You're the sane part of me," Vann said.

"And you're the irrational, frightened side of me, Sir. But times like this... We know from our escape we have to become different people. What we'd normally do doesn't apply here. Think like Wickland, become harder, a man without mercy. It's the only way it'll work."

"I know, but—"

"We can't save the pack with doubts in our minds, Sir. Think of your parents, of Terena, the rest of the pack, and those poor cubs—my half siblings..."

Kip's words helped to bolster Vann's reserves. He plowed on, more determined than ever to do his part. They continued for a time without communicating. Vann studied the rest of the group and how they all seemed intent on reaching their destination, running full tilt, muscles rippling beneath their coats, tongues hanging from the sides of mouths under their bag straps. This was something Vann had never experienced outside his family unit or while he was with Kip. Solidarity, each member resolute in working together to achieve their common goal.

Had those at Highgate been brought up to fight for every pack member? Did they class themselves as one big family? Vann thought back to how it had been there, with Sergeant at the helm and those strange circles the Highgaters had formed when faced with adversity. They'd enclosed their quarry, standing shoulder to shoulder.

Yeah, they're a huge family all right.

The pack at Crossways was a divided bunch, each family keeping themselves to themselves, hardly ever coming together. Trust was a massive issue—no one had much of it—and hiding feelings was normal. Could the Crossways shifters be saved as a group, or would Vann have to work around them, dealing with each secluded cluster in turn? He suspected the latter would be the case, and that might hamper things a bit. Time was of the essence, and they couldn't spend much of it messing around with several explanations that would be repeats of the ones that had gone before.

No, I'll have to be strong and order them all into the community room.

He wanted to laugh at that. Community room? Since when had there ever been a sense of community at Crossways? Had there ever been, before Bennett's rule? And how had Bennett become the alpha anyway? Had he bided his time, acting as though he was the right one for the job? And once he'd secured his place as their leader, had he changed? Had life at Crossways been like it was at Highgate once upon a time?

He didn't know and had no spare minutes to ponder it now.

Crossways was in the distance, and changing direction so they could approach undetected was the next thing on their list.

Chapter Six

Kip felt no apprehension whatsoever now. Revenge burned deep in his heart, and the one thing he concentrated on was freeing those cross-bred cubs, along with anyone else who wanted out. He wondered, as he loped through the woods surrounding Crossways with the Highgate group, whether a new alpha would be chosen once Wickland and his cohorts were apprehended and taken away by Alpha Newart. Or would everyone be encouraged to go into institutes, as was first discussed? It seemed crazy to abandon Crossways, leaving a perfectly good compound vacant. The windows, blank panes with nothing beyond, would be a creepy reminder of what had gone on there—empty lives and messed up shifters. Couldn't some pack members stay, change things up a bit, remodel the place so it didn't resemble Crossways any longer?

Memories will live on in the walls, though. Maybe a clean break is best for all who live there. A new pack could take over, shifters with no emotional attachment to it—bad emotions, ones that can cripple a person.

Kip had only lived at Crossways for a short time compared to the others, but he hated every inch of the place. His mother had been killed there, right on the lawn in front of everyone. A lesson to pack members that if they had it in mind to piss Bennett off, they'd meet their maker the same way.

Could I live there knowing my mother's blood has seeped into the soil? And on the other hand, could I leave, knowing a part of her is on Crossways land?

She hadn't been buried like normal people, as a whole person. She'd been eaten, so there hadn't been anything to inter. But there were bones, picked clean by evil wolf teeth, tossed into a hole in the woods on the other side of the compound. Could Kip just go, abandoning them for good? They were still his mother, still something that had been her.

What would she want me to do?

Kip didn't have to think for long.

She'd tell me to go wherever the sun shines in my heart – and that'd be with Vann. So where he goes, I'll go.

More settled now that he'd thought things out, Kip ran with extra determination. The trees thickened, and it wouldn't be long before they maybe encountered one or more of the Crossways guards in wolf form. But if the Highgate group had played it right time-wise, they might not encounter any.

Ahead, Dillon came to a stop then shifted to human form. The others halted in front of him. One kept to the side, a meter or so away, and scanned the trees. Kip and Vann remained at the rear. Vann brushed his muzzle against Kip's. The movement was welcomed and much appreciated, confirmation that Vann was there for him, as always.

Dillon hunkered down to pull his watch from his bag. "We're early," he whispered, putting his watch on. He drew the strap tight and winced. "I want this on so I avoid shifting again until I have to. Didn't want to wear it on the way here in case I lost it. You all know it has a GPS tracker inside so Alpha Newart and Sergeant can see where we are at all times. When I do shift again, we'll approach our entry point as we've agreed, but we'll wait until the guard has passed. No moving until I give the signal."

Kip nodded along with the other wolves.

"And, Vann, Kip, you know what needs to be done." Dillon shifted again then strode to the wolf who was still observing the woods.

They took the lead together, slinking between trees, their bodies low. The others mimicked them, and Kip took it upon himself to do the same. Adrenaline spiked in his system, and he resisted the need to run fast, to reach Crossways and get things over and done with.

'Nothing good ever comes from rushing, Kip,' his mother used to say. *'Unless you need to get your butt away from danger.'*

She'd told him to run when Bennett had captured her—there had been danger right there—but he wouldn't have been able to anyway. His instinct was to stay with her, to protect her, and the timeframe he'd had to escape had been minimal. Within seconds Bennett's men had gotten hold of Kip too, and the rest was history.

'No use re-reading the last chapter when a new one is right there, waiting for you to turn the page and dive into it. Live it.'

Another of her sayings, one he intended to heed now. It was just sad that her last chapter had been in a horror story no one should have to star in. A Stephen

King epic that would chill readers and make them keep the lights on at night.

But a new chapter was indeed ahead for Kip, although the previous pages of the book that was his life still lingered in his mind. How could he completely forget what had happened? It wasn't possible. Oh, he'd told Vann he could stop himself thinking about things, but he didn't, not fully. Thoughts and memories still hung around even now, when the cubs were eight years old and the remaining parts of his mother had nestled beneath the Crossways soil for all that time. The ache of missing her had diminished, but it would always be there somewhere.

He needed to practice what he preached to Vann and stop thinking of things he couldn't change. It wasn't the right moment to take a painful trip down the lane that led to his former days. He had things to do in his mother's memory, to make it so that her death hadn't been in vain. Vann's victory in saving the pack would also be Kip's. They'd share it, raising their trophy high for all to see.

Focus on the here and now.

The trees thickened even more. They were almost at the entry point. Dillon and his companion stopped. They sat between two trunks and waited for the rest to join them. Kip cursed his white coat, how it stood out in the darkness compared to the other wolves' fur.

If I'm spotted, me and Vann will have to start our performance a little differently to what we'd planned.

Dillon lifted his paw to read his watch. He stared at Vann and nodded.

Kip's sudden nugget of fear was eclipsed by his need to see this through.

Vann glanced at Kip, jerking his head. Kip went with him, to the left, where a path meandered through the woods and led to the Crossways' drive. Vann poked his head out into open space, looking this way and that. He yipped quietly, and Kip understood — time to do their part.

They shifted, slung their Taser bag straps over their shoulders then stepped out onto the drive. Vann gripped Kip's wrist in a show for whoever watched on the monitors — hopefully Wickland, if he stayed true to his usual nightly pattern. Vann strode with purpose, while Kip dragged his feet, pretending he didn't want to return to Crossways. It was easy to act that way. He'd been acting his whole time at Crossways, so now wasn't any different. He mused on how quickly he'd gone back into his old role. How just being here had sent him back to being how he used to be.

At the main gate, fashioned from ancient, rusty iron railings attached to a perimeter fence of the same metal, Vann said, *"We do exactly as Dillon advised unless Wickland or his men try to fuck us over."*

"Yes, Sir."

Vann jabbed a fingertip onto an intercom button that had been screwed to one of the thicker gateposts. It had been put there to be used by delivery men, who dropped off food and whatnot — to keep others out and ensure the pack remained secluded.

A crackle came from the speaker, then shuffles, as though Wickland was pacing his study.

"Look what we have here," Wickland drawled. "The wanderers return. I wondered when you'd be home."

His voice had Kip fighting off waves of revulsion.

"I need to speak with you, sir." Vann bowed his head in respect then lifted it.

Kip felt Vann's spark of annoyance at having to show reverence to the new leader of Crossways. Wickland would be watching them on one of his screens, so Kip didn't dare glance at Vann. Their charade was underway, and the rest of the Highgate group would be about to climb through the opening in the fence about now.

Please, please let them make it in safely. I hope Wickland talking to us is enough of a distraction that he isn't looking at the other monitors.

"What, you need to speak to me out there, in the nude?" Wickland laughed, phlegm rattling. "No, no. You must come in, of course you must. What kind of alpha would I be if I let one of my pack stay outside like he wasn't welcome?"

One of my pack... Kip wasn't considered a proper member, and it didn't hurt him to have that confirmed by Wickland only classing Vann as a Crossways shifter. Besides, it worked well with their plan.

"I wouldn't want to be one of your stinking pack, anyway," Kip shouted, glaring around to find evidence of a camera so he could gaze right into it. He found none. "Never have done. Your brother brought me here against my will, killed my mother, and all I had to do was wait until I could get away without being caught. It took me eight years, but I got out, didn't I? Proves Bennett's rules and his so-called secure perimeter were easily broken." He directed a look of hatred toward Vann. "And will you get *off* me?"

He tried to tug his arm from Vann's grip but Vann held on.

"Shut up," Vann snapped at Kip. "You need to learn to keep your mouth shut. Show some respect to my alpha." Then he said to the intercom, "I've brought him back, sir." Vann yanked Kip to his side. "Like Alpha Bennett would want me to. Kip here escaped the other night and I followed him. I know I broke the rules by doing that but I didn't have time to let anyone know. I apologize for that." He paused, taking hold of Kip with a tight hand on the back of his neck. "Kip runs fast—it took a while for me to catch up to him, that's why I was gone so long. He made it to some place called Highgate, but I caught him there. And I've heard some terrible news, sir. About your brother, our wonderful leader, while we were at Highgate."

"He is no longer leader, Vann, I am." Wickland chortled, clearly unfazed that his brother had been captured. "But I'm glad to see you know where your loyalties lie. Come through. Bring him to my study. I'll tell the guards to leave you be. I'd like to deal with Kip myself. Without interference."

Vann's internal sigh of relief gusted through Kip. They'd made it over the first hurdle. Kip wasn't fool enough to think they had this in the bag, not yet, but hope sprang inside him, and he transferred it to Vann to give him some hope of his own.

The gates swung open, a gaping mouth that would swallow them whole before closing, trapping them in Crossways' belly. It was an eerie sight and thought. If things went wrong and they didn't make it out of here…

We'll make it out. We have to.

Stepping onto the main Crossways compound almost had Kip turning around to run away again. It brought back so many memories of the night he'd first arrived. Determination to do the right thing stopped him, though. There were others to think about besides himself and Vann. Deserting the other pack members would be a heinous thing to do, although Kip could understand anyone else just running and running, never turning back to rescue those left behind. Life at Crossways was hideous. Anyone in their right mind would choose freedom with no guarantees of a good life over incarceration here. Better to struggle elsewhere than suffer, dignity stripped, under the rule of a mad man whose only goal had been to satisfy himself and what he wanted. Wickland would be no different than Bennett, Kip was sure of that. His blasé reaction to Bennett's capture proved the man had no feelings. If he wasn't loyal to his brother, he'd be loyal to no one. A hard alpha to live with.

He'd be worse than Bennett as a ruler. I dread to think what the pack has gone through since he took over.

Kip thrust his meandering thoughts away. He walked into the main house beside Vann. They were greeted by an ominous silence, no sign of guards or any pack members. That was unusual. Someone was *always* in the foyer manning the front door. Yes, Wickland had said he'd tell the guards to leave them alone, but to have no one present at all? Was this how things were done now? New alpha, new rules?

"Don't do what I just did, Sir, and think of life here as it was before we left. Wickland's in charge now. Things could be very different."

"I know. I'm uneasy that there are no guards lounging about in here. Even just one. I expected to be stared at, berated, poked with those canes they always carry."

The canes. The guards were generous with their use of those, smacking shifters as and when they pleased, for fun or admonishment.

"It'd be a different kind of use, the way we'd do it if we had canes, Sir."

"Kip, switch your mind back to the job, for fuck's sake."

Duly chastised, Kip sent a wave of apology to Vann as they neared Wickland's study door. Vann returned it with one of his own—for snapping. Kip brushed it off—no need for them to get wrapped up in their feelings at this point.

Vann knocked on the door.

"Enter," Wickland said, his voice just as loud as it would have been if the door was open.

They stepped inside. Kip was immediately hit with the scent of angry male—a man hiding his emotions behind a cheerful smile. Could Wickland smell their apprehension? Wickland tipped his head to one side, and Vann jostled Kip to a burgundy leather, button-studded chair that spoke of cigars and brandy in a bygone era. Kip sat, wedging his Taser bag between his outer thigh and the seat. The chair was in a darkened corner, and he hoped he'd be able to open the zip without being spotted.

"You can sit over here with me," Wickland said to Vann. "Away from that traitorous son of a bitch." He went to the door. Standing so he could see Vann and Kip, he locked it then pocketed the key. "Now, we won't be disturbed, which suits me fine because I can deal with this infringement of the rules on my own. Having the guards in here will just muddy the waters, don't you think?"

Vann nodded and took a seat at Wickland's desk. "I don't want to be seen as telling you what to do, sir, but you might want to sit down."

Wickland smiled, his grin wide and menacing. "Oh, really?"

He moved to stand beside Vann, and a frisson of uncertainty flickered through Kip. Vann was worried, Kip felt it, but wouldn't anyone be in this situation? Kip slid his hand into the Taser bag. He closed his fingers around the phone in case he needed quick access to the 'off' button.

"I'll indulge you, Vann, but really, I know all there is to know about Bennett." He sat behind his desk, suitably hemmed in.

Things were going according to plan, and Kip prayed it would continue this way. It was as if they were in a play and Wickland had read the script. The man was a cunning bastard, though, so Kip braced himself for Wickland to do a bit of ad-libbing, saying the wrong lines, making the wrong moves, throwing the rest of the cast off-kilter.

Kip could only hope the finale turned out as they expected.

Chapter Seven

"So tell me your version of events," Wickland said, pulling a cigar from a wooden box on the desk then lighting it.

Kip would have laughed if the situation wasn't so dire.

If Wickland pours a brandy next…

A thick puff of gray smoke streamed from Wickland's mouth, rising and churning in the air, a snake in the grass that dissipated to nothing within seconds. A snake much like the man who had blown it out.

"Like I said, sir, I followed him to Highgate." Vann, with his back to Kip, jabbed a thumb in Kip's direction. "Once we were there, some guy called Sergeant got hold of us in the woods. You ever heard of him? And his mate? Bossy son of a bitch. Sergeant called Alpha Newart to tell him we'd arrived and were strangers. I didn't tell them I had a brother in their pack—I thought you might like to deal with him yourself. But the runt is there, I saw him. His name's Jace. Got a cross on his chest. The Crossways cross, so he belongs here, not with those Highgate assholes, right?"

Wickland nodded, seemingly impressed with Vann's apparent dislike for Jace and those at Highgate. "Continue."

"Anyway, next thing I know, Bennett arrived. Said he'd come to take us back home. I was so relived. I can't tell you how pleased I was. I told him I was glad to see him, that I'd chased after Kip and I can only hope he was proud of me. Then that Sergeant guy and his shifters turned up again. They surrounded us, put Bennett's wrists in cuffs then took us to their pack house. Held us hostage in their dining room. Alpha Newart was called. There was a meeting with him, then Bennett was taken away."

"I see." Wickland blew out more smoke and eyed Vann through the miasma between them. "What would you say if I said I'd heard a different tale?"

"A different tale? Who the hell does he have feeding him information, Kip?"

"I don't know, Sir, but we'll have to let Dillon know."

Vann widened his eyes. "I'm not sure why anyone would tell you something different, sir. I'm your loyal servant. I'm here, aren't I? I did what was right and brought that son of a useless whore home."

"God forgive me, Kip. I'm so sorry I had to say that."

"It's all right. I understand the need to seem authentic. Keep going, Sir. You're doing good."

"Hmm." Wickland narrowed his eyes then closed them.

"Get the Taser out, Sir. Quickly."

Vann eased the zip back. Kip coughed to disguise any sound.

"My smoke bothering your little friend, Vann?" Wickland asked, leaning his head back and keeping his eyes shut.

"A little, sir, but it's okay. He doesn't mind." Vann took the Taser from the bag. His hand shook.

"I wouldn't care if it did bother him. I was just making what some might say was polite conversation. Making sure my guests are happy. But then *you're* not a guest, are you. You're family."

A dysfunctional family.

"Yes, sir, I'm family all right." Vann held the Taser under the desk.

Kip glanced at the bank of monitors sitting on a long sideboard beside the door. *"The others are in, Sir. Approaching the house now."* He returned his attention to Vann's back.

"I have plans in place to get Bennett back here where he belongs." Wickland opened his eyes.

Kip's heart stopped for several seconds. He moved only his eyes so he could look at the monitors, hoping Wickland couldn't see him very well in the darkened corner. No wolves were on display.

"They must be in the bushes on the right-hand side of the building, the ones that are flush to the house wall, Sir." Kip watched Wickland puffing away, the air thick with smoke so Wickland appeared shrouded by ghosts.

"Thank God for that." Vann coughed. "May I have a glass of water, please? We haven't had any food or drink for hours."

"Hmm. Hours." Wickland stubbed his cigar out in a gold-colored dish. He stood, crossing his arms over his chest. "That's what's bothering me. It must have taken days to get to Highgate — it's over the other side of Texas — so how did you get back so quickly?"

Vann took a breath to fortify himself for what was to come. "We hitched a ride, sir. And you're going to go on quite a ride yourself."

He stood, his legs a little unsteady, and brought the Taser up to point it at Wickland's belly. Wickland didn't have time to bolt or even blink. Vann fired the Taser, and Wickland staggered against the wall. His body shook, his eyes bulged more than usual, and he let out a garbled sound. Vann stared, rooted to the spot, unable to believe he'd tasered his new alpha. A part of him reasoned it was wrong—the ingrained part of him that had been brought up to respect his leader no matter how he'd been treated—but the other part rejoiced. He clung onto that euphoria as Wickland slumped to the floor, a jittering mass of a man who'd created so much fear inside Vann as he'd grown up that Vann was instantly apprehensive.

"No worrying now, Sir. We had to do this." Kip was at Vann's side in a second, phone out.

He jabbed a message, presumably to Dillon, and Vann just stared at Wickland, wishing his brain would kick into gear and he could do what had to be done next.

"Snap out of it, Sir! I can see the others on the monitor. They're fighting with guards at the rear entrance. As wolves—it could get nasty. Hurry!"

Vann shoved away his inability to move, forcing himself to the other side of the desk so he could bundle the curly Taser wires into a heap then go on to the next stage. A medal hung from a hook on the wall, one Bennett had apparently won as a cub. Vann grabbed it, intending to use the material necklace part to bind Wickland's wrists. He knelt, hating having to touch the man, even though the scar-faced bastard was now out for the count. Once he'd secured

Wickland's wrists, he stuffed the Taser into his bag then took out the phone.

He sent a message to Alpha Newart, who responded quickly, assuring Vann that his men, Marcus and Robert, among others, were on their way. A touch of relief gave Vann the courage to reach down and get the door key out of Wickland's pocket and the bunch hanging off his belt loop. He could free the cubs now, spring open the padlocks that had ensured those children could never escape.

If we make it down into the basement.

The sounds of muffled yelps and snarls filtered into the room.

"The Highgate men are coming, Sir."

Vann looked at the monitors, more relief pouring into him that Dillon stood outside the study door. His wolf form was so regal, gave off such an air of command that Vann allowed himself to relax. He unlocked the door, and Dillon padded in. He sniffed Wickland then sneezed.

"Cigars," Vann said.

Dillon wasted no time ushering other wolves in with a flick of his muzzle. They each took a piece of Wickland's clothing in their mouths then dragged him out into the foyer. Vann and Kip went with them, Kip with his Taser in hand ready to zap anyone who got in their way. At the basement door, Vann sorted through the keys, judging which one fitted the lock. It took several attempts before he found the right one, but once he had, he swung the door wide. Dillon went down the stairs backwards, tugging Wickland over each step. With five Highgate wolves helping, once they'd reached the bottom Wickland was placed in an empty cell. Vann found the right key for that on the first attempt. He locked Wickland in, staring at him through the bars.

He couldn't believe they'd managed this. It took a few seconds for it to sink in. Never in his life before he'd left Crossways would he have thought anyone would have the guts to overpower Wickland or Bennett, let alone sling them in a cell. It was surreal, as though he'd dreamt the whole thing. Or *was* he dreaming? Was their escape and return here just one long dream and he'd wake any moment to find his mind had played a cruel trick on him?

Shit. Please don't let that be what this is. Let it be real.

He studied Wickland again, convincing himself that however real his dreams had been in the past, none felt as real as this one. The man was a heap on the cement floor, resting in the fetal position. Vann felt no sympathy, just pure hatred as he thought of all the things Wickland had put the pack through as Bennett's head of security. Wickland deserved no mercy, and an emotion streamed through Vann, one so strong and alien it made him catch his breath.

I want to kill him.

"That's my fault, Sir. My feelings have been transferred. I'm afraid I feel no remorse for that man. If I could, I'd get in there and maul him to death like he mauled my mom. I feel the same about every single one of them who helped kill her. I should turn the other cheek, like I told you I could, but I can't seem to make these feelings go away this time."

"They're so dark, Kip. They're not like you."

"I've kept them hidden. They weren't meant to seep out, Sir."

Dillon appeared in human form beside Vann, swiping away the chance for more silent conversation. Vann turned to him, his back to Wickland—*I can't stand to look at that bastard anymore.*

"One of our teams has spoken to your father, who directed us to the people on Wickland's side, the ones who would rule here in Wickland's absence if they got the chance," Dillon said. "Your father said only five men were truly loyal to Wickland as far as he knew — our other men should be bringing them down here shortly." He glanced around the basement. "Where are the cubs?"

Dread pooled in Vann's belly. He looked around in the murkiness. All the other cells were empty. He'd been so intent on securing Wickland he hadn't thought to check the cubs before.

Shit.

"I don't know." Vann grimaced. "They're usually always here."

"I suspect Wickland knew something was up." Dillon frowned.

"He said, when he let us through the gate, that he'd call his guards away. I thought it weird that no one was in the foyer. That must have been why. He had his men down here, taking the cubs elsewhere. Him saying he wanted to deal with me and Kip by himself was bullshit."

"So there are more men loyal to Wickland, not just five like your father said?"

"I don't know. There must be. But maybe the ones taking the cubs only did so because they were told to. I'll speak to my father and find out, but if he said only five, I'd believe him. If there are more, then they've obviously kept their feelings on the subject to themselves. Possibly pretended they're on their fellow shifters' sides all these years so they could get information to pass along to Bennett or Wickland."

"Any other places on the property they're likely to be?" Dillon stared at Vann hard. "Come on, man.

Think. They could be long gone by now—not even at Crossways!"

"Fuck." Vann's mind went vacant in his panic to come up with a suitable answer.

He was saved by Wickland's five men being dragged down the stairs by the rest of the Highgate wolves. Vann opened Wickland's cell then stepped back so his unconscious cohorts could be dumped inside with their evil leader. They formed an unruly pile, and Vann got immense satisfaction from seeing Wickland squashed beneath the others.

But was that his feeling or Kip's?

"Mine, Sir. I hope he suffocates to death."

"I never thought I'd say this about someone, but I do too. How can we not think these things after what we've been through because of them? Try not to feel guilty. They certainly felt no guilt when they treated us the way they did. They enjoyed it, I'm sure of that."

Vann sent out a wave of love to Kip then locked the cell, thankful for the first time that the bars were close together to prevent escape. Dillon went to the bottom of the stairs. He switched on a light, which bathed the basement in such harsh illumination that Vann had to blink while his eyes became accustomed to the change.

"Vann's father is gathering the rest of the pack now," Dillon said to everyone. "We have a new job to do, one we didn't anticipate. We have to search every property on this compound. The cubs have been moved." He looked at everyone in turn. "As with our usual missions in the past, we spread out—you know the drill. Vann and Kip, because you're not familiar with how we work, go to the community room and help your father explain things to the rest of the pack."

Vann nodded, eager to see his parents and Terena again.

"Tell everyone what their options are," Dillon went on. "Also tell them Alpha Newart's men will be here shortly, Newart half an hour or so after that. If anyone gives you hassle, bring them down here to be on the safe side. Once Newart is here, he can deal with discovering who's good and who isn't." He lifted his chin. "Now, we have work to do. Find those goddamn cubs."

Dillon shifted then took the stairs swiftly. All but one of the wolves were hot on his tail. A dark brown wolf sat outside the cell containing the men. He flicked his head at Vann, who took Kip's hand and led him from the basement.

In the foyer, Vann paused to gather his strength and wits. Everything had happened so quickly he needed a moment to breathe and process. The adrenaline rush had seen him through the events so far, but now a wave of fatigue took hold of him. His limbs weakened, and his mind didn't appear to want to work. Everything was blank in there.

"Come on, Sir. We're almost there. I can feel it."

Vann shook himself alert, forcing his body to move. They ran to the pack house. Pausing on the porch, Kip sniffed the air, cocking his head, then shifted to his wolf form. He slid his Taser bag strap into his mouth.

"I can smell the cubs, Sir."

Vann was torn between doing as Dillon had asked and waiting for Kip to let him know which direction he thought the cubs had been taken.

"Dillon said they'd search every property," Vann said. *"So we should do what he told us and – "*

"They're not in any of the apartments or the pack house, Sir." Kip trotted a short way over the lawn. *"They went this way."* He looked over his shoulder at Vann.

There was no need for Kip to say another word.

Vann shifted. He scooped up his bag strap then went to Kip's side. *"Which way?"*

"Over there." Kip loped ahead, nose to the ground.

Vann felt Kip frowning.

"There's nothing over there but grass, Kip, and it doesn't lead to the road. All that's there is fucking land and lots of it."

"Maybe they got picked up by a vehicle beyond anywhere we've been allowed to go before, Sir. We have no idea what else is over there. Don't forget, when we were given permission to run, we weren't to go far."

"In which case, it's pointless us wasting time running that way."

"It isn't. I can feel them close, Sir. Please, they're my family."

Vann picked up his pace behind Kip as the white wolf streaked ahead. If Vann didn't hurry, Kip would be so far in the distance it'd take Vann a while to catch up. He couldn't allow his mate to do this alone. And if Kip said those cubs were out this way, then Kip would be right.

He usually always was.

Chapter Eight

Kip sniffed. The smell of the cubs increased. They were here somewhere, out in this vast patchwork of land. In the far distance he could just make out guard wolves on the perimeter of Crossways land — maybe they were unaware of the Highgate men taking command. They appeared calm. He couldn't tell from where he was which wolves they were or whether they were loyal to Wickland. Vann and Kip might have a problem if spotted.

About one hundred yards ahead, the terrain changed. It was flatter, no grass wafting in the breeze. Kip hadn't been out this far before — no one on Crossways was allowed — so he squinted to try to see clearer. Yes, there was definitely a difference. Kip went closer, slowing, wary of what he'd find. Vann caught up, panting hard.

"What the fuck is that?" Vann asked.

Kip gave a shrug and stared at a circle of rough cement. At its center, a smaller metal circle had him frantically trying to work out why it would be here.

There wasn't a padlock in sight, so he assumed the door—it had to be a door, right?—was open.

"Some kind of doorway, Sir?"

Vann slid to the ground then shifted to human form. He turned onto his back. *"I saw guards. You'd better get down on the ground."* He dug into his bag to pull out his phone. Prodding the keys, he grimaced. *"Letting Dillon know we're here. I'm not going to open that hatch until he responds."*

Kip saw the sense in that and hunkered down, waiting patiently—if getting antsy and wanting to investigate that opening was classed as patient. The cubs' scent was so strong here that the hatch couldn't be airtight. They were beneath that metal circle, he was certain of it.

Vann's phone bleeping had Kip snapping his head around.

"Dillon and some others are on their way." Vann put the phone away. *"He said to go ahead but to be careful. I'll have to open the hatch. No way you can do it in that form."*

Kip wanted to whine in frustration. *"Very well, Sir."*

Vann soldier-crawled toward the hatch. Kip joined him. Vann tugged at a metal loop, wincing at the loud grating noise when it turned and scraped against the surrounding iron it was attached to. The sound echoed into the night. He glanced toward the pacing wolves. They hadn't heard a thing, it seemed. Vann lifted the door a bit. Yellow light spilled out, creating a corona.

He lowered the hatch slightly. *"Those guard wolves might see the light when we open it fully and go in."*

"Tough. Dillon's on the way. By the time we're down there, help will have come. I smell them stronger now, the cubs. They've been brought out here, no question." Kip nudged Vann's arm. *"We need to look inside. To see if I*

have to shift to be able to get in. If there's a ladder, I might find it difficult like this."

Vann looked at the guards again then lifted the hatch higher. *"We're okay. It's a few stone steps then a ramp going deeper underground."*

How the hell hadn't the Crossways pack heard about this place? Then again, why would they have? Bennett had many secrets, and if he'd told those loyal to him to keep their mouths shut about a secret underground location, they would have.

Vann fully opened the hatch, cursing the harsh blast of light. The guards would see it, yes, but so would Dillon, giving him and the others something to head toward. Kip stuck his nose over the edge. He sniffed, getting a strong whiff of his half siblings and the heady scent of mold. Without waiting for Vann, he plunged into the hole.

"Wait, will you?" Vann called.

At the bottom of the steps, Kip, frustrated and wanting to get moving, stood still. *"Please, Sir. Hurry."* His body twitched with his need to *do* something.

Vann entered. He closed the hatch then wedged himself by Kip's side.

"There isn't enough room for both of us, Sir. Single file."

Vann moved to go first.

"No. I'll go first," Kip said, surging onwards.

The narrow aisle stretched on for a few meters. Bare light bulbs were spaced intermittently, their wires decorated with fluffy, thick cobwebs. The walls were crudely plastered with cement, or something close to it, the top half damp and green in parts where drips of moisture had dribbled. At the end of the aisle, a steel door barred their way. Kip's heart sank. What if it was locked?

At the door, relief flowed through him at the sight of it being ajar. He nosed it open, conscious that wolves might be on the other side, ready to pounce. There was nothing but a room, empty, its walls built from red house bricks. Someone had spent a lot of time creating the hidden place. Kip cocked his head, keeping alert for sounds and smells that meant danger.

There was nothing but the cubs' scent laced with the mold.

A tunnel mouth gaped opposite, black, the space beyond so secret it gave Kip the creeps. He glanced at Vann, then, before he could be stopped or change his mind, Kip plunged into it. An instant melody of water drips, amplified by the confined space, played a tune that he thought might haunt him forever. It was melancholy, a maudlin introduction to a dank, dark passageway that didn't seem to lead anywhere.

As he went on, the light from behind faded until blackness encompassed him. It was absolute, and walking blind was an eerie experience. He slowed, testing the ground for any hidden drops or steps before he trusted himself to move farther forward. Vann's breaths seemed overly loud, meshing with the water tune and threatening to send Kip into madness. It was like this place was enchanted or haunted by unseen beings that had the intent to stop anyone from reaching whatever was ahead.

Kip bumped into a wall ahead of him. He sniffed, cocked his head again then on instinct, pushed with his forehead. A chink of light spilled into the passage, a gap created by a section of the wall moving inwards. Kip stared through at a room made from the same house bricks as he'd seen earlier. Cells lined the wall opposite, a sleeping child in each one. A black wolf dozed on the floor in the center.

"They're here, Sir. As well as a guard. I think it's Caleb." Kip spotted a lighter patch at the end of the wolf's tail, a black paintbrush dipped in white paint. *"Yes, it's Caleb."*

"Caleb? What the fuck would he be doing here? He hates Bennett and Wickland."

"You know as well as I do that no one disobeys here. He'll have been told what to do. We'd have done the same whether we liked it or not."

Nudging the wall again, praying it didn't make any noise, Kip created enough space for him and Vann to go through. Kip went first, padding in as silently as he could. Vann came to stand by his side. They stared at the kids.

"Drugged?" Vann asked.

"Probably, Sir."

A strong urge to wake Caleb swept through Kip. He dropped his bag so it slapped on the floor then he shifted. Quickly getting out his Taser, he stood beside Caleb, surprised the noise he'd made hadn't roused him. If Wickland had been here and found Caleb like this, dozing when he should have woken at the slightest sound, his life wouldn't have had many seconds remaining in it.

Toeing Caleb in the side, Kip waited for some kind of response.

Nothing.

"What the fuck?" Vann let his bag go, shifted to wolf form then pounced on Caleb.

Taking a mouthful of his scruff, Vann shook his head, growling with anger.

"What are you doing, Sir? Why be so rough?"

"He needs to wake the hell up. We could be anyone. Those cubs could be at risk because he's such a lazy bastard and won't wake up."

Caleb opened his eyes and sprang to all four feet, shirking Vann off, blinking in what Kip could only assume was confusion that Kip and Vann were there. Then fear took over, widening his eyes and raising his hackles.

"It's okay," Kip said, holding out his Taser hand. "Crossways has been secured by good shifters. But if you make one wrong move, I'll use this. And it'll hurt, understand?"

Caleb's hackles went down then he shifted. As a human he looked a wreck. His blond hair, full of grease, hung limply against his scalp. His usually handsome face bore signs of stress—gray shadows under his eyes and deep crevices either side of his mouth. He appeared older than his thirty-odd years— thin, weak. So why had he been chosen to guard the cubs? He was hardly packing any brawn—or strength, as far as Kip could see.

Caleb frowned. "What do you mean by secured? And why the hell have you come back when you got away? Are you crazy?"

"We brought back some shifters from Highgate—it's another shifter compound the other side of Texas. Wickland's been put in a cell. Alpha Newart will be here soon to take him away." Kip smiled, hoping it would go some way to relaxing Caleb.

"Who's the next in line to be alpha here?" Caleb asked, jamming his hands into his hair.

"I have no idea," Kip said. "But it won't be any of Wickland's followers, not now Alpha Newart is involved. Maybe one will be elected. It depends on what the pack wants to do."

"What do you mean?" Caleb eyed him warily, lowering his arms to his sides but bowing them out as if ready to fight if he had to.

"Everyone except Wickland and his followers are free to leave." Kip smiled again. "Can you believe that? We're finally free."

"Free?" Caleb looked like he might collapse. He staggered to a wall, propping himself against it.

"Are you all right?" Kip asked.

Caleb shook his head.

Kip went on, hoping to give Caleb something else to think about other than his apparent distress. "There's room at the institutes, maybe some other compounds if they're willing to take people in. We don't have to stay here if we don't want to." Kip felt for the man and wondered how he'd react in the same position given the same news.

I wouldn't believe it.

"I promise you, you're free," Kip said.

Caleb slid down the wall, and Kip had the inane thought that the rough brick would have scuffed his skin. Caleb drew his legs up, thighs to chest. He rested his forearms on his knees then lowered his head.

"I don't know what to do," Caleb said. "I've lived here all my life. Going elsewhere... It's too frightening."

Kip understood all about that. "But once you step off these lands and see what else is out there — it's amazing. As you know, I've done it. I've seen the way we're supposed to live, before and after I came here. A new life is ahead of all of us. It's yours to take. Or you could stay here with anyone else choosing to do the same thing. I'm sure if people want to stay, Alpha Newart will appoint a good alpha. Maybe even you."

"Kip...there's a — " Vann said.

"Not if I can help it," a man said.

Kip spun around to face whoever had spoken. He should have known it would be him looming in the opening. Wickland's right-hand man, Foster, glared at Kip. Why hadn't he noticed Foster hadn't been captured by Dillon's men?

Damn it!

Vann lunged forward, attacking Foster, paws on the man's chest. The momentum sent Foster backwards. He slammed into the wall, eyes wide in his shock of actually being challenged. Kip stared at his Taser, his mind going blank on how he was supposed to use it. A simple thing like pressing a button eluded him for a second. His brain kicked into gear at last and he pointed the weapon at Foster, poising his thumb over the button, but he didn't have a clear shot. Vann's body covered Foster, no part of the man visible except for patches of arms, legs and his head.

"*Get off him, Sir!*" Kip shouted.

A blur of movement to Kip's left then a shove to his side had Kip reeling to his right. Caleb had shifted into a wolf. He leaped at Vann, wrenching him off Foster, his strength had clearly returned tenfold. Vann rolled backwards, smacking into the wall where Caleb had been sitting, a yelp of pain echoing around the room. Kip wanted to go to him but everything was happening too fast.

"*I'm okay,*" Vann said. "*I'll be okay.*"

"*Just keep out of the way if you're hurt, Sir.*"

Caleb had Foster by the throat. Foster flailed, his arms waving up and down, then he screamed, the garbled sound so full of agony it gave Kip the shivers. Kip stood rooted, unable to fire the Taser without hitting Caleb. Foster slid to one side, down the wall until he smacked onto the floor. Caleb went with him, snarling as he bit deeper. Then he snapped his head toward Kip, ripping out Foster's throat.

The silence was deafening.

Sickened by the gory sight, Kip went to Vann, who was sprawled on the floor panting.

"My leg," Vann said.

"Shift, then shift again. Quickly, Sir, while you have the energy."

Vann closed his eyes as Kip stepped back to give him room. Vann shifted to human form, his leg bent at an angle no leg should be bent in. Vann's face, pale and sweating, scrunched up in his pain.

"Again, Sir. Now!"

Vann took a deep breath, opened his eyes to stare at Kip then shifted again. His howl was heartbreaking as his broken bone knitted back together, but it was the only way to heal. With a brief glance at Caleb to make sure he wasn't intending to harm them, Kip returned his attention to Vann.

"So tired," Vann said.

"I know, Sir, I know." Kip went down on his knees to stroke Vann's flank, watching him carefully for signs of shock. *"Rest for a moment. That's all you need, just a moment."*

Sounds of approaching wolves and the scent of Dillon tore Kip's concentration from Vann.

"The Highgate men are here, Sir. It'll be okay — everything will be okay."

Kip stood then went closer to the opening. He spotted Dillon and the other wolves. "The wolf in here with us is a trustworthy man as far as I know. Caleb. He killed Foster, one of Wickland's men."

Dillon filled the room with his presence. The other wolves remained behind him. Dillon shifted, the top of his head almost touching the ceiling.

He stared around, widening his eyes a little at the blood spatter, at the torn-out throat sitting on the floor. "We caught a few other guards out there on the perimeter. We'll need to do a head count once we're back at Crossways to see if any got away." Dillon looked at Foster. "He got what was coming to him, I take it?"

Caleb growled.

"He did," Kip said. "Caleb's understandably angry. Confused." He hunkered down, placing a hand on Caleb's head. "These are the good men I told you about, Caleb. They won't hurt you."

"If Bennett and Wickland weren't being dealt with by Alpha Newart," Dillon said, "I'd kill them myself for what they've done to this pack. Those children..." He walked over to the cells. "They'll get help. With your consent, Kip, Alpha Newart will probably want to take them to a hospital institute. I suspect Vann's father will want to go with them, to work on some kind of medicine that will ensure these children can shift, something they've never been able to do because it hurts them too much. Or maybe Aaron might be able to create something that will take their pain away if shifting isn't possible."

"Whatever is best for them," Kip said. "If it means they can lead happy lives, then they must go wherever Alpha Newart sees fit." Kip swallowed. "I can visit, get to know them, something that's been denied me all these years."

Dillon nodded. "Then let's get this crap sorted. The sooner the better."

Kip couldn't agree more.

Chapter Nine

Vann stared at his parents and Terena. They stood opposite him in a row in the living room of the only home he'd known. His mother, a slight woman with black hair coiled into an elegant chignon, had tears in her eyes and held out her arms. He went to her, feeling like a cub again, except their size roles had switched. Instead of his head resting on her chest, hers rested on his. His father came to Vann's left side, Terena to his right, and their family circle was complete.

"Oh, son, I can never thank you enough for what you've done," his father said, his voice rusty. "The nightmare is over."

"And you found my boy, they said?" his mother asked, her words muffled within their embrace.

"Yes, and he's a fine man," Vann said. "They called him Jace, and he has our cross. He looks like me, only smaller." Vann paused for a moment, remembering Jace and what he was like. "I didn't get to know him much while I was there, but he's willing to meet us all. I think." He worried how to word what he had to say next but decided to get it over with. "You have to remember, though, he's been brought up in a completely different lifestyle, by two men who dote on him. Don't expect too much."

Their circle loosened.

His mother looked up at him. "I understand, but…I can't wait to see him. To know him."

How could Vann let her down gently? How could he help her to understand that just because she loved Jace, even though she'd never known or held him, Jace might not feel the same way about her? She was a stranger to him, a figment, Vann suspected, of Jace's imagination.

There was no other way but to just come out with it. "I know you love him because he's a part of you, but… His mother—his other mother—isn't a female, you get that, right? Dillon, the man heading the Highgate group? It's him. Jace isn't used to females in his immediate life, so you and Terena will possibly have to tread carefully. Be his friends rather than his family at first, yeah?"

She nodded. Swallowed. "I'll be whatever he wants me to be."

"Good." Vann smiled, relieved she'd taken the news well. "And he has a mate. A man he's known since childhood. Louie. So your only chance of grandchildren is with Terena." He laughed, pleased to see that bit of information didn't matter in the slightest.

Their bonding moment had passed, and each of them sat in their usual places—parents on the sofa, Vann and Terena in matching chairs.

"What will you do now?" Vann asked, looking at his father.

"We were hoping to remain here, son. I have my medical supplies, my lab, all I need to work to help the children." He shrugged. "But if they want me to go to one of the hospitals and live at another institute, that's what I'll do. I owe it to the cubs to make things right." He sighed. "I'll never forgive myself for what I allowed to happen."

"It wasn't your fault," Vann said. "We were trapped here."

"I wish we'd..." His mother stared out of the window, eyes glazed.

"Stayed free?" Vann finished for her. "But you didn't, and that wasn't your fault either. Being captured, brought back here... It was all out of your control. No one blames you. It's like Kip saying he should take the blame because his mother gave birth to the cubs. It doesn't work like that. They were forced to come here, his mother was...forced to go with that lion. What's done is done." He smiled at Kip's saying.

"Where is Kip?" his mother asked.

"Visiting the children at the pack house. He's trying to explain what happened and what the plans are for the future." Vann scrubbed his chin. "Alpha Newart has brought a psychologist with him. She's also with the cubs—she'll know how to help them understand. It'll be a long process, like it will for everyone who lived here, but we'll all get through."

"You were victorious, son, as I knew you would be." His father grinned widely. "You saved us all."

"Not just me. Kip...I couldn't have done it without him." Vann reached out mentally to Kip then, asking if he was all right. "One second." He held his hand up to let his family know he was tuning in.

"The children are very receptive, Sir. It must be their youth, but they seem to understand that life will get better

for them. One has attached herself to me and says she wants to be called Scarlet."

Vann felt Kip's happiness, his relief that everything had worked out okay. Who would have thought their escape would bring this about? Yeah, they'd hoped—hoped so goddamned hard—but had never quite believed they'd pull it off.

"Good. Maybe everyone will be just as receptive." He pushed his love toward Kip.

"Not Caleb, Sir. He'll take a while. He can't imagine leaving. He's frightened of what's out there."

"Then maybe Alpha Newart will appoint him as alpha—Caleb has the heart and fire for it. Or he will have once he's gotten over the shock. He was always so strong, so sensible. And he loves this place."

"Dillon said something similar, Sir. And Caleb's family want to stay here, as do others, except the majority are excited to catch the bus to the city and get jobs, live a normal life. It'll all turn out right, you'll see."

"What will we do? Where do you want to go?" Vann asked.

"Wherever you are, Sir. The location doesn't matter."

"Highgate?"

"If that's where you'll be happy, Sir. That's all I care about."

Vann staved off the burn of tears. Kip was his life, his everything. Without him…

"Okay, I'll see you shortly, Kip."

"Bye for now."

Vann gave his family his attention. "We'll be going back to Highgate with Dillon and the others," Vann said, looking at them one after the other to see if they'd object. "I loved it there, and Jace… I want to be with him, to go back so he doesn't feel abandoned again. He needs to know we're there for him, even if he doesn't want to become too attached. I just…need to do this."

His mother smiled. "So you'll watch out for him until we can come to visit? If you're there, I can rest easier if we have to move from here. Who knows what hospital institute we'll be at if Alpha Newart prefers your father to do his work elsewhere."

"I will." Vann stood. "I'm off now to meet with Dillon to let him know our decision. Sergeant, that's Jace's father" — he gave his dad an apologetic look — "said we're welcome, but I'd like to make sure."

"They sound like good people," his father said. "Thank God Sergeant was the one to find Jace on the road. If he hadn't—"

"But he did," Vann said. "And he's a great man, honest and kind. You'll get along well with him."

Vann left after another family hug, making his way toward the main pack house. It felt strange to actually be wearing clothes again. Other than the trip from Highgate to Crossways, he hadn't been dressed in ages. There was something about walking without the encumbrance of material that made him feel good.

I could get used to that…

"I don't think the Highgate pack would appreciate you strolling round naked, Sir. When shifting it's natural. No one takes any notice, but all the time?"

Vann laughed quietly. *"I wasn't planning on it in public, but in private? Yeah, I could go with that. You?"*

"I'd be quite happy to parade in front of you without clothes on, Sir. You should know that already. It's something I've looked forward to from the moment I fell in love with you."

"I know, it's the same for me. What are you doing now?"

"I'm on my way to my room. There's nothing else I can do for the cubs. They're busy with the psychologist, who seems to have fallen in love with them. She's a single woman and

made a point of saying she's willing to adopt if that was needed—not the usual practice but there you go. I'm happy about that. They need someone like her. So I wanted to gather some clothes if we're moving to Highgate."

"May I join you after I've spoken to Dillon?"

"You may, Sir. I'll wait for you. Naked."

"That can wait until the hotel room, or when we get back to Highgate."

"Spoilsport..."

Vann laughed again, loudly this time, then immediately stopped, glancing about to see if anyone was there to hear him. Then he realized it didn't matter if they were. He could do what he liked now. It seemed surreal that he was free on Crossways land, and he understood how Caleb couldn't get his head around the changes. This place held so many memories—negative ones that would only serve to keep Vann from being his true self if he let them remain in his mind. The air held an oppressive quality, as though the breeze contained eyes that reported his every move. Even if those eyes were only in Vann's imagination now, he couldn't stay here. He'd forever be looking over his shoulder just in case things switched back to how they'd been before.

He reached the pack house and went inside, following the sound of Dillon's voice. He found him in the community room with Alpha Newart and his men, Marcus and Robert. Dillon sat casually naked, as if it were the most natural thing to do.

Alpha Newart stood, and Vann dipped his head.

"Hello, sir."

"Be seated." Alpha Newart gestured to one of the free chairs then sat back down. "I'm pleased you're here. I didn't get the chance to thank you properly at

Highgate for what you've done. Your determination to save a whole pack warrants a medal."

"It's nothing, sir." Vann's face heated. To be praised by their overall leader wasn't something he thought he'd ever see. To meet other wolves from other packs wasn't something he'd really thought would happen either.

"Nothing?" Alpha Newart smiled. "Modesty—I like that in a wolf, which is why I wanted to offer you the position of alpha here."

Vann blinked, his stomach coiling into knots. Would he have to accept? He wasn't sure how these things worked. Were there rules in the shifter world where if an alpha position was offered a wolf had to take it no matter what? The fear of having to remain here rose up in him, and he knew he wouldn't be able to lie or accept gracefully. "I'm very flattered by your offer, sir, but please, if it's possible, I'd like to decline. I can't..." He looked around the room, searching for the right words to say. "I can't bear to stay here. My life...it was a prison sentence, one I got to spend with my family but a sentence all the same. The thought of being here for the rest of my life isn't something that would make me happy. I wouldn't rule as I should. I'd be constantly wishing I wasn't here."

"I understand." Alpha Newart reached out to place a hand over one of Vann's. "The position was an offer, not an order. Perhaps, having lived here all your life, you might have a suggestion as to who would be suitable? As you must understand, Crossways has been kept secluded and I've had no access that would allow me to get to know the people here. I wouldn't want to choose the wrong person."

"Caleb," Vann said without thinking. "The wolf who killed Foster. Kip, my mate, said Caleb is frightened of leaving Crossways. It's all he knows. And there are others who apparently want to stay. He's always been a good man, was a good cub while we were growing up."

Alpha Newart nodded, taking his hand away. "Then I'll talk to one of the older shifters to find out some information on him before I offer him the job. I assume Caleb has been here your whole life?"

"I don't recall a time he wasn't here," Vann said, "but that's not a guarantee he wasn't brought in when I was too young to remember."

"Okay. If the information I receive about him is to my satisfaction, I'll ask him. I'd appreciate it if you'd keep my plans to yourself for the time being—sharing them only with Kip, as I wouldn't expect you to shield something from your mate. That wouldn't be right. Thank you for your help in this matter—and for being honest." Alpha Newart smiled. "What will you do if this land makes you so uncomfortable? Where will you go?"

"That's what I came here to ask." Vann looked at Dillon. "If it would be possible, could me and Kip go to Highgate with you?"

Dillon grinned. "Of course. You have family there."

"Thank you," Vann said.

"Will you ever come back here?" Alpha Newart asked. "If, say…your parents were to remain?"

"No, sir. I would arrange to meet them elsewhere."

"Are they amenable to leaving Crossways?" Alpha Newart raised his eyebrows. "I'm asking you because I don't want to cause them any more distress. Your father's role in all this was a terrible tragedy, one I suspect will stay with him for the rest of his life. Heaping more demands on him at this time isn't something I'm prepared to do if he's fragile."

"They'll go wherever you want them to be, sir. My father just wants to put things right."

"Good, then I shall offer them a home elsewhere. I had news from the psychologist that although the children are already coming on in leaps and bounds, they would fare better in a different environment. The upheaval of moving in circumstances like this is generally deemed to do more harm than good because the children are used to it here. But they've voiced wanting to see the ocean, and I'd hate to deny them when there's a perfectly wonderful hospital institute right by the sea." He nodded absently. "Of course, I'd need Kip's consent, and he will have to sign papers because they're his siblings. What are his feelings on all this, do you know?"

"He's the same as my father. He wants what's best. If we can visit the children from time to time? Kip would like to get to know them."

Alpha Newart beamed. "This is all working out so very well. Yes, you're welcome to visit whenever you like. With your parents at the same place, a great time will be had by all, I'm sure. Perhaps Jace would go with you?"

Vann looked at Dillon.

"Jace is…" Dillon rested a finger across his chin. "Jace is a difficult person to understand. He may need time, but I'm sure in years to come…"

"Yes, yes," Alpha Newart said. "That boy has had a lot to come to terms with. As we all have. But there are brighter days ahead, ones filled with sunshine."

Hope soared anew inside Vann. He'd take sunshine any day over the dark, repressive days of the winter his life had been so far.

Chapter Ten

Kip felt Vann's awkwardness. They were back at Highgate, arriving with just the clothes on their backs and a few in a holdall each. Jace walked across the lawn toward them in wolf form, having just scarpered from the oak trees. Louie was with him, Jace seeming subdued now he'd spotted Kip and Vann. Hadn't news spread of their coming to live here?

The wolves approached, Louie with a loose-limbed gait, Jace all stiff and bristly. At the porch, Louie shifted then moved to the clothes bin where everyone stashed their things before shifting. He dressed with his back to them, quickly, turning once he'd gotten his jeans and T-shirt on. Jace remained as a wolf, staring at Vann as though he considered him an intruder. There was some kind of accusation in his eyes, or maybe that was apprehension?

Louie came to stand beside Kip. "Look, he doesn't mean to be so...aloof. He's got a lot on his mind and he's trying so hard to be a better person. Just give him time, all right?"

"We didn't come out here to…" Vann shrugged. "We were just on our way to your old apartment when you came running out."

Kip nudged Vann, back to their old way of doing things now the mission was over. Vann nodded his permission for Kip to speak.

"We can stay away from you, if you want," Kip said, looking at Jace. "It's hard for you, we understand that. Hard for us too. We need to adjust to living somewhere that allows us freedom. We've been living a life where being monitored is normal. As you can imagine, adjusting will take a while." He smiled to show he and Vann meant no harm. "We're all having to adjust but in different ways. So we get it, we really do. Vann will wait for you, Jace. It's on your terms — you getting to know each other, I mean."

Jace nodded, walking to stand beside Louie. He pressed into his side. Kip realized Jace was feeling vulnerable, probably torn between shifting and speaking to them or running away, pretending all this newness had never happened. Maybe Jace didn't know *what* to say, considering he'd kept his thoughts and emotions to himself all his life.

"We're all a bit of a mess in one way or another," Vann said. "Time — I heard it's a great healer."

"It is." Louie reached down to ruffle Jace's fur. "Already Jace is coming out of his shell. He's opening up a bit more, mainly with me, but in the future, who knows? He'll maybe feel more comfortable with you guys."

"I'll wait for as long as you need me to, Jace." Vann looked up at the sky then back to Jace. "And even if you don't want to become friends or meet your other family, it's okay. Whatever you want. I get it. Our parents and sister also understand. They just want what's best for you."

Jace stepped forward. He cuffed Vann's leg with a splayed paw, snarled, then ran off toward the apartments. Vann stared after him, and Kip sensed he was crushed by the gesture.

Louie laughed, throwing his head back and holding his belly.

"Why is that funny?" Vann asked.

"I'd say you've got the seal of approval," Louie said, smiling hard, his eyes bright.

"How so?" Vann frowned. "From where I'm standing, he just warned me to stay the hell away."

Louie shook his head. "He didn't. That was his way of telling you he wants to be friends. He did the exact same thing to me when I first met him. From then on, he spent years wanting to be with me, to play as cubs, to be friends, then later, mates. But he kept it all inside because he didn't know how to express himself. It wasn't until you showed up that he told me how he felt. The thought of being taken away with you, back to where he was supposed to belong, freaked him out. So he told me he loved me, and, well…you can see how it is now."

Vann's relief poured through Kip, who laughed with the euphoria of it.

Vann joined in, staring in the direction where Jace had gone. "I thought… Fuck, it doesn't matter now." He turned back to face them.

"Just wait," Louie said, "and he'll come to you." He patted Vann on the back. "Honestly, it'll all turn out okay in the end. Anyway, I'll catch you later. There's a wolf I need to see to. Oh, and enjoy it here. You deserve a good life."

Louie walked off. Vann looked at Kip, his smile infectious. Kip returned it, knowing their time here would be so very different than what they'd been used to. Kip could still remember life from before Crossways, how it was to mix with the fulls as though they weren't a different breed. Vann, though...he had a lot of new things to experience, and Kip supposed in a way Vann wasn't much different to his brother. The siblings both had adjustments to make, new patterns to get used to, and maybe once they'd come to terms with those changes in their own lives, in themselves, they'd eventually broaden their horizons to allow some kind of brotherly relationship to grow.

"It'd be nice, wouldn't it?" Vann asked. *"Permission to answer me."*

"It would, Sir, but like I've said before, talking in thoughts isn't necessary here. Unless you have something outright private to say." Kip gazed at him, a challenge to make Vann start understanding that their relationship didn't have to be kept a secret anymore.

"It's so difficult, though." Vann clenched his jaw then relaxed it. *"For all the time you were at Crossways we spoke in thoughts once we'd mated. If Bennett had known for sure about us..."*

"I'd have gone the same way as my mom. Yes, I know. But I didn't, and now we're here." He lifted his arm to encompass the compound. "We never have to hide again. So talk to me out loud, Sir. Please?"

Vann stood a few inches away. He looked as if he wanted to take Kip in his arms, but the habits of the past were intruding, stopping him from doing so.

"Hold me, Sir. In public. Right now where anyone can see."

"Fuck. I want to, I really want to..."

"So do it."

Vann swallowed, tilting his head toward the sky. *"It's...it's so embedded in me that I..."* He smacked a fist against his thigh. "I love you, Kip." He snapped his head down to stare at Kip then glanced around. *"Fuck, I said it out loud."*

"You did, Sir, and it sounded lovely. Say it again? Louder. Shout it?"

Vann bit his bottom lip. His indecision was right there for Kip to see in Vann's darting eyes and him changing his hands from fists to star shapes.

"I love you!" Vann shouted. He shut his eyes, cringing, probably expecting Bennett or Wickland to come storming from the pack house ready to eat him alive.

"No one's here, Sir." Kip grinned, ecstatic he'd gotten Vann to loosen up so quickly. "Take a look?"

Vann opened his eyes a crack. Then wider. "Jeez, this is so weird. I feel...I feel alive. Like I've just been born."

"In a way you have, Sir. A new life, a new you. I'm going to enjoy the journey we'll be taking."

Vann stepped closer, tugging Kip into his arms. Vann's heart beat wildly beneath Kip's ear, and Kip sensed the elation skittering through Vann as though it raced about searching for somewhere to go, somewhere to escape from. Kip dragged it into himself, fully sharing the emotion, fully understanding the enormity of the pressure release.

"I *love* you," Vann said, stroking Kip's cheek and pressing kisses to his temple. "You have no idea how much I've wanted to be like this, us standing in the open. Yeah, we were alone when we came here the first time, but that was different. We're in a community now, one that doesn't give a shit what we're doing so long as it isn't breaking the law." He paused, squeezing Kip tight. "We're free. I can't believe we're free."

"It feels good, doesn't it, Sir?"

Vann squeezed him again in answer.

"Shall we go and drop our bags at the apartment then drive into Morgan Creek like we planned, Sir? We need to visit the agency Dillon mentioned – the one where we can apply for jobs. It's all very well being welcomed here, but we need to pay our way. We can't expect the others to carry us for long. What will you do for a job?"

"I'm not sure. I'm not skilled at anything, you know that. Mowing the grass and pruning the hedges at Crossways hardly count as skills, do they?" Vann let Kip go. He guided them across the lawn toward the apartments.

"You could bartend with me. That's something I've always wanted to do. Serving people, making them feel happy. Dillon said there are vacancies at some club or other. It means we'd work nights and get all day to spend here."

"Would I be any good at it, d'you think?" Vann opened the main door to their apartment block. "I'm a bit big. Maybe too clumsy to be working with glasses in a confined space?"

"Maybe there'll be other jobs better suited to you. Come on, we'll dump these bags then go and see. We won't know until we check, and maybe something will jump out at you, grab your interest. Dillon said we can borrow his car, and I haven't driven in ages, not since Bennett left his car unlocked and I taught myself. It's time to start our new life."

* * * *

The drive to Morgan Creek was exhilarating. Kip hadn't gone long distances before, and navigating the road with limited experience was a stupid thing to do. He realized that all too late, but he slowed and concentrated, hoping to get them to the small town in one piece.

The countryside between the compound and the town was beautiful, not that he had much chance to study it properly. Maybe one day they could take a walk out here, perhaps have a picnic in one of the fields, providing whoever owned it didn't mind. There were plenty of trees to give shade, and who knew, they might be able to fuck under one of them if it was far away from the road.

"That would be risky — and you may answer me," Vann said.

"I know it would, but risks hold appeal. Like the one in the hotel room with that guy outside. It was exciting, wasn't it?"

"It was, I can't deny that."

"So we'll go alfresco one day, Sir?"

"If that's what you want."

"Oh, I want."

There was no more time for conversation. They entered the town and Kip had to concentrate on driving. He managed to park out the back of a supermarket. How Kip would reverse when it was time to go was another matter, one he didn't want to think about until he had to.

As Kip and Vann strolled along the main street, people watched them, curious, Kip thought, as to who they were. It wasn't because they were shifters, more that they were strangers. Well, he and Vann were here to stay, so these folks would just have to get used to seeing them on a regular basis.

It was strange, being among fulls again—being among anyone who didn't belong to Crossways or Highgate—but Kip would soon adjust and he was sure Vann would too. Although it had to be harder for Vann, whose feelings flowed through Kip, one chasing after another.

Kip patted Vann's arm.

Vann nodded.

"No one will come along to take you back to Crossways." Kip smiled. "So there's no need to look around for anyone who might seem menacing."

"I can't help it. I can't believe I'm walking down a street with you. Such a simple thing. These shops and that little patch of a market down there. It's all so...like it's on TV and I'm just watching." Vann stared around in wonder. "And shit, I just realized. We're here to apply for jobs yet we have no identification papers."

Kip dug into his jeans pocket. "What, like these, Sir?"

Vann stopped walking to take them. He studied them for a moment. A birth certificate each and a piece of paper that had social security numbers on it. "Where did you get these?"

"Dillon gave them to me. Alpha Newart provided them. Which reminds me, we have to find a photo booth. We need passport photos. But more than that, we can do what all new couples do and get some dorky pictures of us messing around."

"New couples do that?" Vann raised his eyebrows and handed Kip's birth certificate back to him. He slid his own into his pocket.

"Well, they used to when Mom was younger, so she said. She had some of her and my dad." Kip shrugged. "When they were happy. There's so much you don't know—so much I'm going to enjoy watching you learn. There really is a whole new world out there, Sir."

Vann swallowed. "Does it make me sound stupid if I say I'm crapping myself about going into that agency?"

They continued walking.

"No. It makes you sound human." Kip laughed. "Or as human as you can be, anyway."

"And fulls really don't mind shifters being among them? Like, there isn't any fear or prejudice?"

"Of course there is. Some people don't like what they don't understand. There are assholes wherever you go, whether you're a full or a shifter. And many people hate gays, so according to some we have two things against us. Just go with it. We'll muddle through any bad times." Kip spotted the agency sign swinging in the breeze on the side of a building. "Here we are, Sir."

They stopped outside.

Vann read some of the cards in the window. "Farmer's hand wanted on the other side of town. Reckon I could do that? It says here 'Help needed with mucking out pigs and cattle'. Shoveling shit can't be that hard, can it?"

Kip laughed. "It's your call. Personally, I want a cleaner job. Cleaner than a bartender anyway. One where I can maybe wear a suit. I've always wanted a suit."

"Then I'll get you one with my first wage packet."

"You don't need to do that, Sir."

"But I want to."

Kip raised his head so he could look at Vann. The need to do it had been fierce inside him, and he wondered whether Vann had put the thought into his mind. "Don't you like me always looking down, Sir?"

"Not always, no. Sometimes I just want to look into your eyes, you know? To make contact for a second. Maybe we can relax that rule now. I mean, it worked so well at Crossways, when you felt you had to *not* look at me, but in this life? There's room for it if you want it."

"I don't mind. Whatever you want. Always, whatever you want." Kip smiled brightly, his heart light and his mind full of future possibilities. "So, after you, Sir." He held out a hand to indicate the door. "Time to start living."

Chapter Eleven

Vann's legs ached something fierce. It reminded him of when they'd walked across Texas, except that seemed like a lifetime ago now. Six months of living free had seen him get used to normal living pretty quickly. He was surprised at how fast he'd become accustomed. Working at the nightclub, Mistrals, had helped too. He'd encountered all sorts of people, some downright bizarre, others more like himself, just people wanting to get on with their lives the best way they knew how. As for the bizarre, who was he to judge anyway? He had no right to question their outlandish clothing and hairstyles, their loud brashness and extroverted natures. Maybe they weren't even extroverts. He'd been so used to folks being quiet and meek, perhaps the rowdy bar goers were average humans.

Whatever, he was enjoying his days spent at Highgate then his evenings and early hours of the morning tending bar with Kip. Like he'd thought, Vann had been clumsy at first, and, if he were honest, nervous of messing up. But Kip, who had taken to the job so easily, had helped him out along the way. And he'd bought Kip that longed-for suit with his first wages like he'd promised, although where Kip would go to wear it was anyone's guess.

The drive back to Highgate in the dark after a busy shift was a welcome rest before they went for it at home with a scene. Kip drove, competent behind the wheel now, and Vann rested his head back and closed his eyes with complete trust in his mate's abilities. The occasional headlight beam flashed over his eyelids, and he marveled at how such a simple thing to some people was still a wonderful novelty to him. Would he ever get used to being free? Ever stop being amazed by new experiences? He hoped not. Losing that feeling meant taking things for granted, and he never wanted to do that.

A light pat on his arm forced his eyes open. Vann glanced across at Kip. He didn't have to give permission for him to speak these days. They'd adapted their lifestyle to match their new style of living, but Kip tended to slip back into their old ways from time to time.

"Sorry, Sir. I forgot I can speak when I want to," Kip said. He smiled in apology. "I was thinking about my suit—your thoughts seeped into my head, sorry. I'll be wearing it next week when I take you out to dinner."

"Will you now. Where are we going? And will I need a suit too?"

"Only if you want one—and we'll be eating at that diner beside the club."

"Won't you look out of place there in a suit? I've never seen anyone go in there wearing one. Seems more like a casual place to me."

"I don't care if I do look out of place. What does it matter anyway? I should wear whatever I want if it makes me happy."

Vann grinned. "See, that's what I love about you. Always looking on the bright side, never letting society dictate."

"It comes from being dictated to at Crossways. Every move monitored, the right to make my own decisions ripped away. Who would continue to live like that if they didn't have to? Yes, Sir, I'm going to damn well wear my suit, and if people don't like it, well, that's just tough. They can stare, comment, whatever they like. I won't care because I'll be with you and doing what I want. Although I wouldn't want to put hardship on another person, it's a shame more people don't have some experience of being controlled or limited. Then they maybe wouldn't judge others quite so harshly for dressing or behaving in a crazy, carefree way. Everyone has the right to be happy, to do what their hearts tell them."

"Then I'll join you. Buy a suit of my own. We can be stared at together. Thought of as the oddballs...the insane Highgate wolves."

Kip laughed. "I suspect some of them would definitely think of us as oddballs if they knew what we'll be getting up to when we get home."

Vann thought of the whip sitting on the chest of drawers in their bedroom. They'd managed to navigate the Internet without too much bother, and Vann had used his newly acquired debit card to purchase a few sex toys. The paddle had been a great introduction for Kip to gauge his pain levels, for Vann to gauge them too. But Kip wanted more. Vann had been uncertain at first—too much too soon?—but Kip had assured him that there was something inside him that pushed for intensity, for a level of pain he would know fitted his needs once he'd experienced it. How was a red raw ass and a hobble for a walk after their last session not painful enough? Kip had tried to transfer his feelings to Vann on the subject, but Vann, not being a pain lover, just didn't understand it. But so long as Kip was content, that was all that mattered.

"A whip in the bedroom isn't exactly everyone's cup of tea, is it?" Vann said.

"No, but it's our cup, and we like it hot and steaming."

Vann laughed at that, looking out of the windshield at the road ahead. Yes, it was their cup, and they were enjoying the freedom of drinking from it.

The turning for Highgate was coming up, and his stomach turned over with his excitement. Although their hours at the club ran them off their feet, Vann still found the energy to fuck Kip afterwards. With everything being so new—sexy things to explore, barriers to pull down, bridges to cross, lessons to learn, trust to cement further—they'd entered a new kind of honeymoon stage in the bedroom. And the things Kip had been thinking lately, well…

His cheeks heated at his thought of the visuals he'd been treated to from Kip only this morning. Vann swallowed and stared down at his groin.

Hard again.

"I wouldn't have told you those things if I'd known they'd affect you out of bed, Sir." Kip flicked the indicator switch then turned onto Highgate land.

"Of course you would have. You gave me those images on purpose because you knew I wouldn't be able to stop thinking about them all day."

Kip smiled. "Is that devious of me—or clever?"

"Clever. Because I've been riled up for hours, and when I get you in that bedroom, your ass is going to be *so* red by the time I've finished."

"Promises, promises, Sir."

At the end of the driveway, Kip maneuvered into the parking area and selected their usual spot. He cut the engine then opened the door so the interior light splashed on.

"You know that whip?" Kip asked.

"Yes…"

"It isn't on the chest of drawers anymore."

"What?" Vann frowned. "Where is it then? Did someone go into our apartment and find it? Take it away?" Surely not. Highgate people respected privacy. Didn't they?

"Of course they didn't. No one else has keys to our apartment, so Dillon said, and I believe him. He's always told us the truth so I have no reason to doubt him. And as for the whip, it's in the woods. By that pond at the clearing." Kip leaned across to nuzzle Vann's ear. "I've decided to take some of the control tonight, if you don't mind?"

"No, I don't mind. What kind of control? What have you been plotting?"

"We're going to shift, Sir. Run. And when we get to the clearing, you're going to whip me."

Vann's breathing quickened. "Jeez. Outside? I didn't mind the idea of doing it in a field off the compound, but at Highgate? Really? With the possibility of other shifters around?"

"They won't be around." Kip licked Vann's earlobe.

"How do you know?" Vann's dick pressed against his jeans zipper. Kip's closeness, his sexiness, was driving him crazy.

"Because I asked them to avoid the clearing from four until six this morning. I said we were going to have a romantic picnic after work and didn't want to be disturbed."

Vann let out a long breath. "What, did you get them all together in the dining room and make an announcement or something? Please tell me you didn't do that."

"No, Sir. I put several words in several ears and let them spread through the grapevine."

"And all without me knowing. Hmm, so you can keep things from me after all."

"Only good things for good reasons."

"So you told them it was for a picnic, huh? I'm glad you said that and not a whipping. I know we're being more open now, but damn, that would have been taking freedom of speech a little bit too far."

Kip tongued Vann's neck. Then he kissed his collarbone at the spot where Kip had bitten him on the night of their mating. "Do you remember that, Sir?"

Vann nodded. "I think back to it a lot. How did we not make a noise with the bond taking over us? It was tough to keep silent, but shit, that night was the best of my life."

"Want to add another to that list?" Kip got out, tossed the keys inside to Vann, then said, "Lock up and hurry up, Sir."

Vann watched him run down the side of the pack house. Kip was so different now, more confident, less subby in everyday life. It was great to see him that way, taking some of the control from Vann, giving them both a bit more freedom to experiment with how they felt and what they needed. At times Kip went right back to how he was before, head bowed, obeying, agreeing to whatever Vann wanted, but other times, like now? Fuck, it turned Vann on in a way he couldn't explain. Like fire burned through him, giving him the urge to follow Kip's lead, wherever he wanted to take him.

And right now it was the clearing.

Vann locked the car, slid the keys into his pocket then ran to the back porch. Kip had already gone, leaving his clothes on the dewy grass instead of putting them in one of the bins. Vann did the same, stripping fast then shifting even faster. He ran toward the woods, exhilaration flying through him as he sped between the tree trunks. He reached the clearing in what seemed no time at all and came to a stop just inside the tree line. He scoured the area, seeing no sign of Kip. The moonlight glanced off something white beside the pool, and he walked toward it.

A piece of paper.

He shifted then unfolded it.

I'm bent over a fallen log, Sir. To the right, where we arrived here for the first time when we found Jace. Come and whip me.

The double entendre wasn't lost on Vann. *Come.* He grinned, ripping the note into pieces then placing the bits into a refuse bin attached to one of the trees. He made his way into the woods, recalling that this was where Jace had subdued Bennett all those months ago. He knew the log Kip referred to, and it was a few more meters in. He walked on, his cock hardening at his thoughts of using the whip for the first time. It was more of a crop, really, like the ones people used on horses. Vann had tried it out on his palm and it had given quite a sting. Giving Kip the same sting on his ass then coming was too much of a temptation to resist.

Ah, there Kip was, bent over the log just like he'd said, ass up, knees digging into the ground. Fuck, what a sight. Vann drew closer, taking in the scene, wanting to imprint it on his mind forever. Kip's skin seemed to glow whiter, despite the shadowy murk of the woods. He stood out starkly against the foliage backdrop, his blond hair hanging forward to obscure his face.

"I hear you, Sir."

Vann smiled. "And I see you, sub. The whip. Where is it?"

"Just there, propped against that tree trunk. My ass needs it so badly. Give it to me hard, Sir?"

Vann didn't answer. He couldn't. What Kip had said stole his ability to speak. He narrowed his eyes, searching for the whip. He spotted it lurching against the tree, waiting for him to just reach out and take it.

He did. It was heavy at the handle, flimsier as it tapered into the actual crop. The end was thin — that was going to hurt like a son of a bitch — and he decided to strike Kip using the center section to minimize the initial bite. He stood behind Kip, staring down at him, amazed at the way Kip was so ready to receive, to be given pain.

"How many strikes?" Vann asked.

"Three. For now. Thank you, Sir."

"Do you want me to spank you first, to get your ass ready?"

"No, Sir. I don't want any numbness from you smacking me. I need the real deal. Please."

Vann widened his eyes, feeling Kip's eagerness to have that whip slap against his skin. He did a couple of test arcs to get the hang of the toy then, before he could back out, he brought it down on Kip's right ass cheek. Kip's head jerked up, and for a moment a shaft of moonlight illuminated his beautiful face. His eyes were massive, his mouth open, lips drawn back. His teeth could have been taken for a feral grin, but that was no grin of malice. Kip was smiling, laughing now as he gripped the log and keened as though he were in wolf form, howling.

Vann's cock hardened further from him seeing the vision of his lover like that, at the sound of him working through the pain, enjoying it, acknowledging it fitted him, belonged to him, something no one else could own, something no one but Vann could give him.

And there it was, the understanding, the reason why Kip needed it. The realization flooded into Vann while Kip let all his emotions go, Vann scrabbling to catch each one as they streaked by. Kip had to have this, something special, something different, and Vann was the only one he wanted giving it to him. That knowledge warmed Vann, turned him on in the extreme. He flicked the whip out again, wanting to watch its journey, see it hit the mark but failing because the motion was too fast. Kip sucked in a breath then released it, gritting his teeth.

"That's what you want, isn't it?" Vann asked, preparing himself for the last strike. "That's the kind of burn you've been after."

"Yes, Sir. Oh, God, yes. More. One more. Harder."

Desperation came off Kip, feeding Vann's desire to please his sub. He struck out again—yes, much harder—then dropped the toy as he fell to his knees. His instinct was to press on Kip's ass cheeks, to take away the burn, but Kip sent him a growl that reverberated inside Vann's head.

"No, Sir. Let me…have this. Let me work…through it. Fuck, oh fuck!"

Kip rarely swore, and hearing him sent Vann's libido skyrocketing. He spied lube down by Kip's knee and soaked his cock with it, enjoying the smooth glide as he moved his hand up and down his length. He tightened his grip as hard as he dared to mimic the feel of Kip's arse clamping around him, but it wasn't enough, wasn't the same.

"Get in me, Sir?"

Vann poured more lube onto his fingers. He drenched Kip's ass pucker then fingered his hole, feeling like he was about to lose control. The tip of Vann's cock was hot, his balls heavy and tight with the load he needed to spunk out. Jesus, who knew seeing Kip getting so much pleasure from pain would send Vann insane with need?

He removed his finger then positioned his cock. He slid in easily, holding Kip's waist to give him the leverage for the kind of fuck that would mean them both toppling from the force. Kip pushed back, his action louder than any words. Vann fucked him hard, the hot skin of Kip's ass cheek heating Vann's upper thigh. And that was the tipping point. Vann started coming, unable to stop it. He took Kip's cock in hand and jerked him off with swift, determined strokes. He went at it in a frenzy, his goal to make them both come hard and fast. Kip moaned loudly, frantically reaching back with one hand to hold Vann's thigh, digging his nails in.

"Yes, Sir! Oh, yes. Fucking *yes!*"

Vann juddered, his orgasm washing through his groin. Kip's dick throbbed then he came, the pulse of cum a steady beat on Vann's palm. Holding his breath, Vann let the final stream of his orgasm jet out of his cock. He exhaled then slowed in Kip's ass and on his dick, until he no longer moved, spent and exhausted from exhilaration. From the quick but incredible ride.

They stayed that way for a short while, Vann getting control of his breathing, thinking about how he'd finally used a whip. Wow, their lives had really turned around, hadn't they? Sometimes he couldn't get over it, didn't believe it was really happening, but other times, like now, he soaked in the pleasure of not only a waning orgasm but the sheer happiness at being able to live life on their own terms.

Kip looked up and Vann followed his gaze. Stars sparkled in a patch of sky visible through a gap in the leaves directly above them.

"You got your fuck beneath the stars," Vann said, leaning across to cover Kip's back with his body.

"I did, Sir, and God, it was heaven. I knew it would be."

Vann smiled, shutting his eyes and enjoying their close moment. He rested his cheek on top of Kip's back, listening to the thud of Kip's heart and his own as they thundered away. They beat at the same time, in tune, as one. As Kip and Vann would always be.

Together.

About the Author

Sydney has always enjoyed writing. "There's something about losing yourself in another world, where the real one ceases to exist and all your dreams and wishes can be placed on the page—dreams for a better planet where love isn't questioned but accepted by all."

When Sydney isn't writing, there's plenty of reading to be done. "I can't imagine not reading every day. It would be weird not to have a book to hand because I've always had one nearby. Life without reading isn't something I'd like to contemplate. The thought brings me out in hives."

Sydney lives in a peaceful area where the hustle and bustle of the city doesn't figure. "I left city life years ago. Too stressful for me. I prefer listening to the swish of leaves on the trees instead of tyres on tarmac. The twittering of birds instead of the chatter of people. Alone time to reflect and ponder is a must. A small portion of every day spent by myself is vital to my sanity and soul."

You can follow Sydney on Twitter.

Sydney Presley loves to hear from readers. You can find their contact information, website details and author profile page at http://www.totallybound.com.

Totally Bound Publishing

Home of Erotic Romance